WITHDRAWN

The Princess in the Pigpen

The Princess in the Pigpen

JANE RESH THOMAS

Clarion Books

New York

Acknowledgment

I'm grateful to my editor, James Cross Giblin, for his
encouragement and direction while I wrote this novel.

Clarion Books
a Houghton Mifflin Company imprint
52 Vanderbilt Avenue, New York, NY 10017
Text copyright © 1989 by Jane Resh Thomas

Library of Congress Cataloging-in-Publication Data
Thomas, Jane Resh.
The princess in the pigpen / by Jane Resh Thomas.
p. cm.
Summary: Elizabeth, a duke's daughter sick with fever, travels
through time from Elizabethan England to a farm in modern Iowa,
where she has difficulty convincing anyone of the truth of her
story.
ISBN 0-395-51587-4
[1. Time travel—Fiction.   2. Farm life—Fiction.]   I. Title.
PZ7.T36695Pr   1989
[Fic]—dc19   89-856
CIP
AC

Q 10 9 8 7 6 5 4 3 2 1

*To Liv Munson-Benson
and to Tunie Munson-Benson,
mother, daughter, sister, friend.*

Contents

1 "What Is This Place?" · 1

2 The Magical Coach · 7

3 "This Doctor Is A Woman." · 15

4 "I'm To Be Shot?" · 26

5 Kidnapped and Ill · 34

6 Ann's Doll · 44

7 The Test · 51

8 The False Queen · 60

9 The Road to Nowhere · 66

10 A Dire Prophecy · 72

11 A Clouded Crystal Ball · 78

12 Charington in Flames · 86

13 Outsmarting Dr. Davis · 96

14 Playmates and Friends · 110

15 A Splinter of Sunlight · 120

16 Reunion · 126

The Princess in the Pigpen

CHAPTER ONE

"What Is This Place?"

"THERE, MISS ELIZABETH," said Sukie, brushing the moist hair back from the child's eyes. "We've sent to the herb woman. She'll bring you something for the fever."

Elizabeth felt herself sink into the featherbed as Sukie pulled the fur coverlet up around her chin. She would soon be warm.

"The fever, the fever," Elizabeth heard the servants whisper, their starched aprons rustling.

Sukie, the nurse, squeezed the water out of a lace-edged handkerchief into the silver basin and bathed Elizabeth's face. The cold water shocked her, but she felt too sick to move away.

"The fever, the fever." She saw Nancy and Martha, new maids-of-all-work from the village, girls not much older than Elizabeth herself, peeking between the blue velvet draperies that hung around her bed. Elizabeth had tried to make friends with them, but Sukie had interfered. The daughter of a duke could not be friends with servants.

"Hush," said an older voice. "Back to work. Her mother mustn't know." That sounded like Mary, the housekeeper, who could sweep everyone but Sukie and Father before her like a broom. The heavy bedroom door clicked shut. It sounded far away.

"I'll undress you in a little while, after you've caught your breath." Sukie tucked the porcelain doll, Mariah, under Elizabeth's arm. She turned the little crank on Elizabeth's music box and, as the song spilled forth, curled the child's fingers around its walnut handle. It played the Summermusic, the air Elizabeth had first heard played from the Queen's river barge last summer on the Thames. The composer Mr. Byrd had created the piece of music especially for the party, a surprise for the Queen.

"I'll be here, my dearie, just outside the curtains, knitting you a warm vest," said Sukie, patting the pocket where she kept her knitting. Her voice sounded cheerful, but Elizabeth saw her cover her mouth with her hands as she turned away.

Elizabeth thought about her mother, deathly pale and bedridden with fever and pain in many joints. "The fever, the fever," she thought.

Puck, the little spaniel dog that never left Elizabeth's side, turned around and around on the foot of the bed and settled himself in the shadows. Then Sukie pulled the heavy blue curtains almost shut. A narrow shaft of sunlight shimmered in the crack between the curtains, fell across the darkened bed, and struck Elizabeth's face. The glare in the gloom stunned her eyes and hurt her pounding head.

In the next instant, Elizabeth heard a noise like the screeching of a rusty hinge. Startled and slightly dizzy, she looked around in wonderment, unable to believe her own eyes and ears and nose.

In all her nine years, she had never seen such a wretched place. An instant before, she had been snuggled under the wolfskin coverlet in her bed. Now she stood with pigs surrounding her, jostling her and crowding toward a trough. The sharp odor of pig manure choked her and turned her stomach. Pigs, here in her bedroom, in one of the finest houses in London? Pigs clambering over one another, threatening to knock her down and trample her? But this was surely not her bedroom.

"Sukie-e-e-e," she cried, but the snuffling and grunting and squealing of the pigs swallowed her voice. She clutched the handle of her music box and tucked Mariah tighter under her arm. Lifting her long velvet skirt with her free hand, she turned to gaze around her. Sukie had just now tucked her up in bed, and she couldn't remember going anywhere. What was she doing in a pigsty?

As she turned about, she saw a man standing in a shaft of sunlight that fell across the dusty room and struck Elizabeth's face. The man looked as shocked and bewildered as she felt. He was clearly a peasant, but not one of her father's servants – she knew them all.

Wiping away the tears on her cheeks with her sleeve, she mustered a commanding voice. "Who are you?" she demanded to know. "Take me back to my nurse this instant, or my father will have you hanged!"

At the same time, the man spoke, like the second lower voice in a duet. "Who are you, little girl, a princess? And what in blue blazes are you doing in there with my hogs?"

Elizabeth's head was swimming. Somehow she had flown from her own featherbed to this byre, where she struggled to keep her footing in a sea of pigs, Mariah under one arm, the walnut music box still pouring out its sweet song in her hand. It was as if no time had passed.

And this bold peasant was questioning her, a nobleman's daughter, in his strange kind of English. Father would certainly have this man killed. Or at least run out of London.

"You're in some pickle," said the man. As he closed a gate behind him and made his way across the pen, the pigs parted before him like the Red Sea. Elizabeth saw that he was wearing rough blue pantaloons and a waistcoat over a tartan blouse. Scots wore tartan — perhaps he was Scottish. He seemed poorly dressed in a foreign style, but his hair was golden and his smile kind.

A runty pig squealed and stood on its hind legs, imploring Elizabeth like a puppy to pick her up. She looked down at her favorite dress. The gold tracery Sukie had embroidered on the bodice and sleeves glittered in the splinter of sun. But wherever the pigs had brushed against her, they had smeared and stained the claret velvet. 'Tis too late now to worry about soiling my gown, she thought.

"Sukie!" she called again. "Puck!" She had rarely in her life been out of Sukie's sight. As her fear mounted with the approach of the man, she cried out louder, demanding obedience. "Puck! Sukie!" Still no dog, no nurse. Here she stood, alone in a byre with a hundred pigs and a shabby peasant, not knowing how she had come there or where she was.

"Hold it, there. I don't bite, or even growl." The peasant picked her up and carried her out of the pigsty, while the music box played on, a feeble tinkle beneath the oinks and snorts of the pigs.

"Where did you come from, you and these fancy clothes?" The man set her gently on her feet and looked her up and down. "And where are your folks?"

"My father. . . ." said Elizabeth, struggling to calm

her queasy stomach and rubbery legs. She took a deep breath and started again. "My father is Michael, Duke of Umberland, advisor to the Queen. Take me home at once!" Waving the music box like a scepter, she almost dropped Mariah in the steaming bucket of feed that stood by the gate.

The man laughed. "And I," he said, one foot on the fence rail and his right hand on his chest, "I'm the King of England."

Elizabeth gasped at the peasant's boldness. "Your head will look down from a pike on London Bridge this day," she said. "What is this place?"

"This? Why this is McCormicks' pig barn, in the state of Iowa. Joe McCormick, king of the pigs, at your service." As he made a little bow, a woman stepped through the open door, with the sun dazzling behind her, making a halo of her hair. "And this here's my queen, Queen Kathy."

CHAPTER TWO

The Magical Coach

"*H*ELLO!" SAID THE WOMAN in a friendly way, peering at Elizabeth. "You must be one of Ann's friends. What kind of trick have you girls cooked up? And why aren't you in school?"

As her eyes adapted to the dusky light of the barn, the woman hesitated, looking closely at Elizabeth's velvet gown and the pearls at her throat. She turned to the man. "She looks like she just stepped out of an Elizabethan portrait," she said. "Her costume is a copy of sixteenth-century style." The woman's puzzled voice made a question of the statement.

Elizabeth's head pounded. The music box was running down. "Fetch Sukie, my nurse," she said. "I think I'm going to swoon."

Kathy helped Elizabeth to lie down on a bale of hay

and settled Mariah safely in the crook of her arm. Elizabeth saw that Kathy and Joe were dressed alike, in rough blue clothes. A woman in pantaloons! she thought. This peasant queen would be stoned to death for daring to dress like a man.

"She's burning up with fever," said Kathy with one hand on Elizabeth's forehead.

The fever. Elizabeth knew she must escape from this Iowa place before she grew too ill to walk. Which London lane or back alley might be called Iowa? She had never heard of such a street. How far would she have to walk to get back home?

"The fever must be why she talks so wild," said Joe. He put his hands in his hip pockets. "I asked her where she came from, but all she could talk about was queens and dukes and having my head on a pike at London Bridge."

"She's out of her mind, of course," said Kathy. "But where did a kid like her learn about heads on pikes? You have to know something before you can rave about it. And where did she get such a costume?" Elizabeth watched the woman studying her dress. "And look at the gold inlay on that music box. And that exquisite doll."

"What's your name and address?" said Joe, kneeling beside her, as a peasant should before nobility. "We'll call your parents."

Call her parents? Elizabeth had already shouted for

Sukie and Puck, but nobody had come. "I am Elizabeth. Daughter to the Duke and Duchess of Umberland, Charington House." She held up the coat of arms carved on the back of her music box and watched them closely. She had heard of kidnappers who held noblemen's children for ransom. She mustn't let them see she was afraid.

"No dukes and duchesses in these parts, Elizabeth. Stick out your tongue." Joe pointed a silver wand at her face, and Elizabeth squinted in its light. "Let me shine this flashlight down your gullet. Does your throat hurt?"

"Past saying. And my head pounds." She clutched Mariah and watched the couple's every move, even though the light that burned in the globes on the ceiling hurt her eyes. "The ague has taken me, just as it did my mother. We must have breathed a draught of night air."

"We'll take you to Doctor Davis, our friend in town," said Kathy, brushing the damp hair away from Elizabeth's eyes. She turned to Joe. "I guess we'd better call Sheriff Cox too. We'll find your parents, Elizabeth, but until we do, we'll look after you. We have a daughter about your age. Ann."

Elizabeth thought of the parade of doctors who had treated Mother's fever. Sukie had let her sit in a corner near the bed, where nobody noticed her. Elizabeth remembered what had happened as if it had been a dream. The first doctor had been a man dressed in black carrying prayer books in one hand and a basket of leeches in the other. The horrible creatures had attached themselves to Mother's skin and sucked – Oh! It was too disgusting to think about.

Another doctor also wore black, with a white collar turned up. He brought a kit of sharp little knives to open a vein in Mother's arm. The blood flowed into a silver basin. This bloodletting would cure the congestion that caused the sickness, the doctor had assured Father. Mother's maid Dinah emptied cups of red blood, shaking her head and pursing her lips and glowering at the physician behind his back.

When these cures had not stopped the fever, Father begged the assistance of the greatest physician in the realm, the Queen's own doctor. He came to the door in the Queen's gold carriage, wearing a black velvet doublet and gold buckles on his shoes and pearl buttons in a line down the front of his waistcoat. His several footmen came behind, carrying books and rosewood cases of equipment. This physician acted like a king, Elizabeth thought.

He clapped his hands, and the footman handed him a vial of rusty powder. This he mixed with wine, which a footman poured down Mother's throat. Then he drove away again in the Queen's gold carriage, with his footmen following.

Oh, Elizabeth remembered it all. Mother had been

deathly ill for three days. Dinah had refused to leave her side, but slept, when she slept at all, on the floor beside the bed. She moistened a handkerchief with the broth the cook had made, and squeezed droplets into Mother's mouth.

When she had recovered enough to speak, the Queen's physician returned with another dose of the rusty powder. Mother clamped her jaws shut.

"Her wits are wandering," said the doctor. "Force the potion 'twixt her lips."

Elizabeth saw Mother spit the medicine back in the footman's face. "My wits," she said, as the footman wiped his eyes, "are here at home. I should rather die of the fever than die of the cure."

Soon Elizabeth heard Father shouting in the hall. The physician shouted back, but he went away, and he did not return. Whispering servants gossiped that now, without her medicine, the Duchess would surely die.

A voice roused Elizabeth from her dreaming memories of home.

"Sorry to wake you, Elizabeth, dear." The woman wrapping her in a blanket was not Sukie, Elizabeth saw with alarm, but Kathy. Once again, she smelled the acrid stench of the pigs and saw the globes of light above her head. She could still hear the animals moving restlessly about.

"We'll have to ditch your pretty slippers," said

Kathy. "They'll never recover from the pigpen, I'm afraid. No matter how hard we scrub, they'll still smell bad. But your doll is safe in your arms. And this." Kathy cranked the music box and put it under the blanket into Elizabeth's hand.

"I've already started the car while you were dozing," said Joe. "We'll wait there; Kathy's calling ahead to the doctor and the sheriff." As he carried Elizabeth out of the pighouse, she saw the runty pig's blunt face thrust between the fence rails as it watched her go.

Elizabeth's fear melted into astonishment. The tree-lined avenues and the green lawns and the noblest houses of London were gone. She had somehow been kidnapped and spirited away to the country.

And what a country! As far as she could see on every side were perfectly flat fields planted in rows of high, pale yellow plants. The fever must have hurt her eyes, for in the distance she thought she saw carriages moving in the fields, drawing enormous wagons heaped with gold. But though she strained her eyes, she saw no animals. The carriages moved as if by magic. She held Mariah close, and listened to the muffled music under the blanket.

"What is the gold in the wagons?" she said.

"Corn," said Joe.

"Where are the oxen?" she asked. "How do the carriages go, with no beasts to pull them and no men to push?"

"Oh, you're pulling my leg, Elizabeth," said Joe. "Or are you a city girl? We've used tractors all my life."

First *flashlight*. Now *tractor*. What were these strange words? And these people spoke English with a foreign accent. Were they Spaniards perhaps? Would the Queen's enemies carry off a little girl?

"The car's around here," said Joe.

Elizabeth looked back at the red byre and ahead at a white cottage. In the dooryard stood another coach, long and low, shiny red, and as beautiful as any carriage the Queen had ever ridden in. One end belched smoke. Across the front, an English word was written. F-O-R-D. Ford. But where were the horses?

Joe opened a door in the side of the coach and laid Elizabeth down on the soft plush cushions. She heard a rumble and felt vibrations. The air was warm inside; might the smoke have issued from the carriage itself? She had never heard of a carriage with a hearth.

Joe sat in the front compartment, and soon Kathy climbed in too. She turned and smiled. "We'll be there soon," she said. "It isn't far."

This woman spoke an English so strange that Elizabeth could scarcely understand her. Just then, the carriage lurched and began to move, even though the ground was level, even though no horses pulled and no servants pushed. Yet Kathy's smile didn't fade; her calm gray eyes never flickered.

Elizabeth sat up. Smoke billowed behind as the carriage gathered speed. They raced faster and faster, faster than any horse could ever go. Elizabeth's heart kept pace, and fear rose in her throat.

My wits are wandering, indeed, she thought. The fever has made me mad. She looked out through the crystal casements. The fields and the roadside trees rushed by at an unimaginable speed, yet Kathy and Joe sat calmly watching the road ahead.

Elizabeth felt dizzy. A duke's daughter mustn't cry, but her eyes filled with tears. A duke's daughter mustn't let them *see* her cry. She lay down on the plush cushions, Mariah's cool porcelain face against her own hot cheek. She turned the crank on the little walnut box, shut her eyes, and held the Summermusic to her ear.

As the music played, Elizabeth imagined the green banks of the Thames on the day of the great party where she had first heard that music. The crowd of splendid ladies and noble gentlemen had played shuttlecock and bowls while the quartet sent its song from a barge anchored on the water.

Elizabeth imagined that she heard the rustle of servants' starched aprons and saw Sukie's smile and her round pink face. But now, she realized, she was speeding with strangers in a magical coach toward an unknown town, sick in body and sick at heart. How would she ever find her way home from such a place as Iowa?

CHAPTER THREE

"This Doctor Is A Woman."

$\mathcal{E}$ LIZABETH HUDDLED IN the back seat of the McCormicks' red carriage and waited.

"This is Ann's school," said Kathy. "Watch that door. That's where the children come out to meet the school bus."

Elizabeth heard the loud clamor of a bell such as she had never heard before, a clamor that went on and on. The school doors burst open with a crash. Out poured a river of children, first the big boys, all of them running, followed by the girls and the smaller children, who were still struggling to find the sleeves of their jackets.

"There's Ann!" said Kathy, smiling. "The girl with straight blond hair, wearing pink shoes and blue jeans."

Elizabeth looked, but blond and pink and blue described half the girls in the crowd. When Kathy stepped out of the carriage and waved, one of the girls ran and caught her around the waist.

"Dad found this strange little girl standing in the hogpen a little while ago." Elizabeth shucked down in the seat as Kathy talked about her. "She's raving with a fever, so we're on our way to Dr. Davis's office. We thought it would be better for you to go with us than to find us gone when you got home."

"Where did she come from?" asked the freckled girl, Ann.

"We haven't a clue," said Kathy. "But it sure wasn't from anywhere near here. You sit in the front — I don't want you to catch whatever she's got. And try not to stare at her clothes." Kathy hesitated before she opened the door. "She's terrified, Ann. Be nice."

"Mom." Ann sounded annoyed. "I'm always nice to kids who are nice to me." She gave Elizabeth an appraising look as she climbed into the carriage. "Hi," she said.

Elizabeth did not reply.

"Okay," said Ann with good humor. "If you don't want to talk now, we'll get acquainted later."

While Kathy climbed into the back with Elizabeth, Joe kissed his daughter. She fastened a wide strap over her shoulder and across her lap, and then he drove away. All across town to Dr. Davis's place, Ann kept turning around for another peek at Elizabeth, whose head now rested in Kathy's lap. The blanket had fallen open; Elizabeth saw Ann look at the front of the velvet dress, and at Mariah.

"Your doll looks just like you," she said. "Do you like to play dolls?" She turned back to her father. "Can she come back to our place? I'd love having a friend to play with."

"We'll have to try to find her folks," said Joe.

Elizabeth tried to ignore Ann's curiosity. She gazed at Mariah with some curiosity of her own, realizing that Mariah was something to cause other little girls to stare. Looking at the doll was like seeing her own image in a mirror. Mother had commissioned an artist to copy Elizabeth's face in porcelain, with the same creamy skin and rosy cheeks. Mariah's chestnut ringlets had been snipped from Elizabeth's own hair.

The dressmaker always stitched a doll's frock that exactly matched every detail of each gown she made for Elizabeth. She looked at Mariah and beheld what Ann's assessing eyes were measuring in Elizabeth's own clothing. The doll's claret velvet dress was decorated with gold embroidery. Tiny pearls were stitched in intricate designs. A lace collar stood wide around her neck, and a string of pearls circled Mariah's throat.

Elizabeth imagined herself for a moment playing dolls with Ann, but she quelled her longing for a friend. She must not make friends with kidnappers.

"This kid must be rich," Ann muttered.

"'Tis not polite to stare," said Elizabeth. She pulled the blanket to cover her dress and hid Mariah in the crook of her arm. Ann wrapped her coarse blue jacket tight around her, as if to protect her mean garb from Elizabeth's criticism. She turned to face forward, and she did not turn back again.

When Joe jostled her awake to carry her into the doctor's lodgings, Elizabeth was dreaming again, of riding in the Queen's carriage. But where were the Queen and her carriage now? Nothing seemed familiar here in Iowa. Kathy and Ann followed after Joe and Elizabeth into a long, low cottage.

A woman dressed in white met them at the door. "Dr. Davis is waiting in there," she said, pointing, "and Sheriff Cox is around the corner, wanting to talk to you, Joe. He's run a computer search through the missing-persons files."

Joe laid Elizabeth on a high table in a tiny crowded room. He nodded at Kathy. "You take care of this end and I'll handle the other." He patted Ann's shoulder gently. "You can stay here with Mom and Elizabeth," he said, and quietly went out.

"Let me help you out of your pretty dress so the doctor can look you over," said Kathy. She supported Elizabeth against her own body while she undid the many buttons down the back of the velvet gown.

The room Elizabeth saw over Kathy's shoulder was utterly plain except for a picture of two rabbits in blue waistcoats, and a porcelain basin with silver spigots. But one wall was painted bright blue, and the door was yellow.

Elizabeth saw none of the ornately carved furniture or tapestries or silver candlesticks that decorated luxurious rooms in London. Yet this doctor must be rich, for there on the wall hung a flawless looking glass where Elizabeth could see her own scarlet face. She touched her cheek to feel its heat with her fingers.

Kathy pulled the dress and then the petticoat over Elizabeth's head, and handed them to Ann. "Here, honey, would you fold these?"

Elizabeth glimpsed herself in the mirror again as Kathy helped her lie down. She and her cousins loved to play with the cheap hand glass that Father had bought them at a London market stall. They moved their faces up and down to make its uneven surface distort their features. First their eyes would look like frogs' eyes, then their noses like pigs', and then their lips like fishes' wide mouths.

Fine people could afford much better mirrors than that. But this physician, who displayed no carved furniture or tapestries, owned a perfect one. Elizabeth sighed and lay back, pulling a blanket over her bare chest and glad for the warmth of her lacy pantaloons.

She was too tired and sick to wonder anymore.

Ann was rubbing the petticoat's tissue-linen fabric between her thumb and finger. "Did you embroider this yourself?" Ann stroked the design of flowers and birds. "I embroidered some pillowcases last summer. How did you learn to stitch such fine work?"

"Our dressmaker is noted for her art all over London." Elizabeth felt too tired to talk, almost too tired to breathe. She went on, however, trying to be civil to these people who had her in their power. "She embroiders my clothes. But I am learning stitches from the Queen."

"The Queen! What Queen?"

Just then the door swung open. "Ah, Sharon," said Kathy. "Here's Dr. Davis, Elizabeth."

Expecting another milk-white man, like her mother's doctor, cloaked in black and carrying a basket of leeches, Elizabeth opened her eyes to another shock. This doctor was a woman wearing a white smock over a tartan skirt so immodestly short that it didn't even cover her ankles. Her skin was as dark as the black-walnut case of the music box. And her arm lay comfortably around Ann's shoulders.

"Sharon and I went to school together," said Kathy.

"Hi, there, Elizabeth. I'm Dr. Davis. Kids call me Sharon or Shanasha. Take your pick."

"What manner of name is Shanasha?" asked Elizabeth.

"Oh, that's a name I gave myself, after I went to

Africa last year. I got tired of being plain old Sharon," said the doctor. "Kind of a fancy, pretty name, don't you think?"

Elizabeth was all the more shocked. She had never heard of anyone changing the baptismal name her parents had given her. How could this woman think of such defiance, much less act so outrageously?

"What a beautiful dress." Dr. Davis picked up Elizabeth's velvet gown from the chair where Ann had carefully laid it, treating it like something valuable. She traced a line of gold embroidery with her dark forefinger. "It's fit for a princess."

Elizabeth stared at the doctor; her teeth were as beautiful as Mother's pearls. All of these people, Elizabeth noticed, had clean and even teeth. At home, even the Queen had gaps where teeth had been pulled.

Kathy stepped back, but Elizabeth reached for her and she came close to the table again.

"Where do you hurt, Elizabeth?" asked the doctor.

Elizabeth pointed to her throat and then to her head, too worn out with astonishment to speak anymore. When she had seen a dark-skinned traveler once at court, a lordly Moor named Othello, everyone had talked of nothing else for weeks. Mr. Shakespeare the playwright had seen the gentleman too, and watched him with great interest. People gossiped that soon they would have a play about a Moor. Here in Iowa, the physicians were not only females, but Moors as well.

"Open up," said Dr. Davis.

Elizabeth watched the physician for a clue of what to do. Dr. Davis opened her jaws, so Elizabeth did the same. She saw Ann open her mouth too, as if in sympathy.

The doctor thrust a wooden stick into Elizabeth's mouth. "Oh, your tongue looks just like a strawberry. We'll do your bloodwork in a minute."

Elizabeth remembered her mother's blood in the silver basin. She looked around for a way to escape, her heart bursting with panic, but there were no casements, and Kathy stood by the only door. The room spun, and Elizabeth held tight with both hands to be sure she would not fall off the edge of the table.

"Elizabeth!" The voice sounded far away. "Elizabeth!"

A dark face floated in the air close to Elizabeth's own. She shut her eyes and shook her head to clear her vision.

"Oh, my," said Dr. Davis, "you're scared, aren't you, honey? You've never seen a doctor like me, have you?"

Elizabeth shook her head, and then the room whirled, and the table seemed to tip. Surely this was a nightmare. She would awaken in a moment. She would laugh with Sukie about the fantastic people she had conjured in her fever dreams.

"Have you ever seen a thermometer before? Have you ever had bloodwork done?"

Elizabeth shook her head. The word *thermometer* was familiar. Elizabeth had studied Greek and Latin with Father for years. *Therm* sounded as if the word had something to do with heat. Perhaps these people were Greeks.

Out of the corner of her eye, Elizabeth saw Ann watching her closely with a puzzled expression on her face. "I've seen thermometers all my life," said Ann. "Haven't you ever had a temperature?"

Temperature? What in the world was a temperature? Elizabeth shut her eyes and shook her head. "Never," she said.

"Here's the thermometer." The doctor put another stick in Elizabeth's mouth. "Close your lips now, and hold it under your tongue."

Elizabeth did as she was told although the stick was uncomfortable.

"Did your doctor ever prick your finger?" the doctor asked.

Elizabeth shook her head again.

"Ann, why don't you stand up here so Elizabeth won't feel so scared. May I hear your music box?"

Elizabeth wound the crank, and the sweet music poured forth again.

The doctor removed the strange device from Elizabeth's mouth. "That's no ordinary toy. The music sounds like an Elizabethan air."

"So it is. I first heard it at the Queen's summer party

last year. A quartet played it from a barge on the River Thames."

"Weird," said Ann.

Elizabeth wondered whether this woman – this doctor – would obey the command of a duke's daughter. "My father is the Duke of Umberland, counselor to the Queen," she said. "Take me to him. He will reward you handsomely for my return."

"Double weird," said Ann.

"We're looking for your parents," the doctor said. "Until we find them, the McCormicks are as good a substitute family as you'll ever meet. The child welfare agency has already agreed."

Dr. Davis rubbed her finger across the carved back of the music box. "What's this?"

"My family's coat of arms." Elizabeth showed her the stag and panther, both erect and facing each other within a border of oak leaves. "The Queen's gift to me for my birthday."

Ann sniffed in obvious doubt.

Dr. Davis turned the music box over and over in her hand, showing Kathy and Ann the carved leaves that covered every surface except for the handle and the silver crank. She looked at the date, inlaid in gold.

"This does look like a birthday present only a queen could afford," she said, staring into Elizabeth's eyes. But the date, Elizabeth. The date is 1600. How did you come by such a precious antique toy?"

"'Twas new, last birthday," said Elizabeth. "And I had it from the Queen." She sighed, tired of repeating her story, tired of feigning patience. These ignorant people could not absorb the simplest facts. Perhaps escaping from fools would be easy. But once she was free, how would she find her way home through such strange neighborhoods as these?

CHAPTER FOUR

"I'm To Be Shot?"

"*H*OW OLD ARE YOU, Elizabeth?" asked Dr. Davis.

More questions. "Nine years," Elizabeth said with a sigh. "I was born on the Queen's birthday, so Father named me for her."

"Which queen, did you say?" asked Ann.

"Queen Elizabeth, of course. Gloriana."

Dr. Davis gave Elizabeth another long and measuring look as she held in her hand a silver amulet attached to two black and silver tubes.

"I can hear your heart with this stethoscope." She showed it to Elizabeth. "Lift your sweatshirt, Ann. This is how it works." The doctor watched Elizabeth as she listened to Ann's chest. "Do you want to hear?"

Elizabeth shook her head and hugged Mariah and gripped the music box. Her stomach churned. Her throat felt raw when she swallowed. Her head pounded like a drumbeat. Let them do what they wished; she was too sick to care.

Ann took Elizabeth's hand in her own. "Dr. Davis always helps me when I'm sick. If she has to do something that hurts, the hurt doesn't last long."

With a light touch, Ann brushed a strand of Elizabeth's hair away from her eyes. "If they can't find your parents, maybe you can live with us," she went on eagerly. "You can go to my school. As it is, the nearest kid lives a mile away from me."

Kid? What did a baby goat have to do with play and school? More confusion. But this plain and freckled girl in pantaloons was kind like her peasant father and mother. Surely they would not kidnap a little girl. Elizabeth squeezed Ann's hand.

Now Dr. Davis listened to Elizabeth's chest and listened again, over and over. Then she took the hand that Ann held and quickly stabbed one finger with a tiny silver lancet. She squeezed a drop of blood from the wound and rubbed it on a wafer of glass. Tears brimmed in Elizabeth's eyes. These people had such strange superstitions. She dared not trust them.

The doctor sat Elizabeth up and took her in her arms. "You have scarlet fever, Elizabeth," she said. "It's a strep infection. See these red lines, Kathy?" Her dark hand moved on Elizabeth's pale chest, indicating the creases by Elizabeth's armpits. "Her red face and the pale circle around her mouth and this rash on her chest and that strawberry tongue all point to scarlet fever."

"Is it contagious?" asked Kathy.

"Yes. Just like strep throat. It's caused by the same germ."

"What about Ann?"

"She was probably exposed to several strep infections in school today without knowing it. We don't quarantine for scarlet fever anymore, since the discovery of antibiotics."

"Oh, dear," said Kathy. "Will she have to take penicillin?"

"Yes. I'll give her the shot myself," said Dr. Davis. She gently helped Elizabeth lie back again and arranged the pillow under her head. "I'll be right back."

Elizabeth clutched the blanket, as if it were a refuge. "Poor Elizabeth!" said Ann when the doctor had gone out. "I had a penicillin shot for strep throat last summer."

"I'm to be shot?" Elizabeth reached out to Kathy. "Oh, I pray you, help me to escape! I did play with the telescope Father brought from Holland. And I took sweetmeats from the cook's stores when she turned her back. But I've done no wrong that I should be *shot* for."

As Elizabeth's words tumbled out, Ann and Kathy interrupted her and each other.

"It isn't shooting with a gun!" said Ann.

"There's nothing to a penicillin – " Kathy started to say.

"Oh, yes, there is! Grown-ups who forget how penicillin feels always tell kids that," Ann said. "It hurts like crazy, but not for long, and it cures strep." Ann hugged Elizabeth. "I bet you'll feel better tomorrow."

"Tomorrow!" Elizabeth wailed. "If she shoots me, I shall be dead on the morrow." She laid her head on Ann's shoulder and wept.

Ann started to laugh, until she saw Elizabeth's eyes. "It isn't shooting with a gun," she said again, more gently, "but a way she has of giving medicine through a needle."

"A needle!"

Dr. Davis interrupted Elizabeth's alarm. She was carrying something small in her hand. It did not look like a gun or an archer's bow, but who could tell in this Iowa, where carriages raced along smooth highways without a horse in sight? Who could guess how a gun might look in this place?

"Hang on to my hands, and shut your eyes," said Ann.

Elizabeth did as Ann commanded, too sick to struggle. She gritted her teeth as well.

"Here we go." Dr. Davis pinched Elizabeth's thigh and swabbed it with something cold.

The pain that swelled in Elizabeth's leg as a howl rose in her throat might have come from a red-hot poker. "Villainy!" she cried. "Shoot me, do, but torture me not!"

"Don't yell in my ear!" said Ann. "And calm down. Nothing's that bad."

"The pain will fade in a little while," said Dr. Davis. "The medicine will protect your heart. And tomorrow you may feel well enough to play." She turned to Kathy in an ordinary way, not with the manner of a woman who would torture little girls. "I'll check her over again when I'm at your place Thursday for dinner."

"Thursday!" said Kathy, combing back her yellow hair with her fingers. "Surely her folks will show up before then!"

She turned to Elizabeth. "Let's just wrap you in the blanket," she said, "and drop off your dress at the cleaners on the way home."

"What shall I wear?"

"I have plenty of jeans and sweatshirts," said Ann, pulling at the baggy pink blouse she wore. "You can wear my stuff."

This urchin actually thought that Elizabeth would wear such rags – Elizabeth, who twice a year spent an afternoon with the Charington dressmakers, being measured and choosing the cloth for her gowns. Only a week before Mother fell ill, she had helped Elizabeth plan her winter wardrobe.

"This sky-blue matches your eyes," Mother had

said, draping a length of velvet near Elizabeth's face as she stood before the looking glass. "And here!" She held up a bolt of rosy wool. "Feel this 'twixt your fingers."

The wool was fine and soft. "It brings out the glints of red in your hair and the roses in your cheeks. Now that you are nine, you may wear lace ruffs like mine," Mother said. "And measure her for a farthingale, Susan."

Elizabeth had smiled. Now when she visited the Queen on Tuesday afternoons, her skirt would billow around her over the whalebone hoops of the farthingale, just like Mother's and the Queen's own gowns.

And Ann was offering to share her rags!

There was a knock at the door, and Joe looked in. "Sheriff Cox wants a word with you, Elizabeth."

She imagined the lordly sheriffs she had seen at court, gentlemen who wore plumed hats and silken hose and gold chains across their bellies. But the man who entered behind Joe wore no plumes, no hat at all. In fact, he had no hair. His head shone like an apple. He wore pantaloons, waistcoat, and sleeves, and a sash tied in a flat knot at his throat, all plain brown, over a white blouse. But on his breast gleamed a large gold medal. It said, "County Sheriff."

Rubbing her aching thigh, Elizabeth saw that Ann watched Sheriff Cox, eyeing something that looked vaguely like Father's pistol on his belt. Elizabeth made herself as small as she could and pulled the little shelter of the blanket up over her chin. Perhaps she had misunderstood. Perhaps it was Sheriff Cox who would shoot her.

"Elizabeth, I need to know a little something about you so I can find your folks," said Sheriff Cox. He didn't sound like a man with execution on his mind. "Your address and phone number. Things like that."

"I am sorry, sir. I do not understand."

"We'll take one thing at a time. Your name and your parents' names?"

"Elizabeth, only daughter of Michael and Margaret, Duke and Duchess of Umberland."

"Address?" When she shook her head in confusion, he added, "Where you live."

"Charington House, London."

"You and your folks are traveling here in the U.S.?"

"U.S.? Joe said this is Iowa."

"Yes, Iowa is in the U.S. The United States, you know. America! The New World!" The sheriff smiled as if he had made a joke.

"America! America is but a savage wilderness." Noblemen at court had talked of America for as long as Elizabeth could remember. But everyone knew that the place was an uncivilized waste, where a wild people spoke a strange tongue.

This Sheriff Cox was mad, but perhaps she could make him see reason. "Sir Walter Raleigh is my father's friend. He it was who sent the colonists to Virginia. Just before my birth." She saw Joe and Kathy exchange glances. "You have heard of the Roanoke Settlement?"

"Give me a break, Elizabeth," said Sheriff Cox. "You ran away, I guess."

This man Cox did not believe her. Nor did Kathy and Joe; Elizabeth could see their skepticism in their eyes. Dr. Davis doubted her too. "No, sir. That I did not. Sukie put me to bed, and the next I knew, I was standing in Joe McCormick's byre."

"Okay. No sense pumping you till your mind clears up." The sheriff opened a kit he carried with him. "We'll get your fingerprints in case your folks had them registered some place."

He began to press her fingers, one at a time, on a pad of ink and then to press them once again on white parchment. What strange customs these people had.

"This paper may help us track your parents down." The sheriff handed her the parchment, where she saw patterns like the swirls she had noticed on her fingertips. "In the meantime," he went on, "I'll call the British consulate in Chicago about this here Charington House. And you and I will talk again tomorrow." He wiped her fingertips with a cold, damp cloth, but she saw that they were still stained.

Elizabeth lay back on Dr. Davis's pillow and closed her eyes on her tears. Tomorrow. Yesterday seemed a hundred years ago. What would tomorrow bring?

CHAPTER FIVE

Kidnapped and Ill

JOE CARRIED ELIZABETH to a bed upstairs in the little house. "Ann's place," he said. "Yours too, for the time being."

It was the attic, Elizabeth saw, with windows on all four walls. At one end stood chests and storage trunks, and at the other were two neat beds, covered with patchwork quilts. The entire top of this cottage was not quite as large as her mother's bedchamber at home. Elizabeth touched a window to be sure the sash wasn't open, amazed by the size and clarity of the panes.

"One of Ann's nightgowns." Kathy handed her a yellow flannel shift. Elizabeth sank back into the deep featherbed and shut her eyes, grateful that something at last felt familiar. But Sukie had always dressed her;

did these people expect her to dress alone?

"Want some help?" Kathy asked.

Elizabeth nodded. Yellow ill-suited her rosy skin, but the shift would do until she could escape and return to her parents.

"Can you walk to the bathroom?" said Kathy.

Elizabeth nodded.

"Ann, you know where the new toothbrushes are. You show her around in there and help her while I start supper."

"I don't want a bath," said Elizabeth, when Joe and Kathy had left. "I need the oubliette."

"Oubliette?" Ann was stroking a big tabbycat that let her hold it like a baby. "Never heard of it."

"Have you then a chamber vessel?" Seeing that Ann still didn't understand, Elizabeth impatiently said, "Chamberpot?"

"Oh, for goodness sake," said Ann. "My dad modernized the farm years ago, when he and Mom bought it. He knocked the outhouse down and filled in the hole. We have indoor plumbing, like everybody else." Ann opened a door near the corner of the room. "Nothing but the best for a duke's daughter." As she bowed, her golden hair fell down around her face. "The bathroom, Milady."

Like all the other rooms in this house, the bathroom was white. At home, people loved the bright colors of jewels and dark oak woodwork. Along one wall of the bathroom stood a great china vessel with odd silver handles at one end and a silver fountainhead on the wall above; perhaps the servants would bring water when Elizabeth felt well enough to bathe.

Ann pointed at a white china chair on the opposite side of the tiny room, which Elizabeth saw had water in its center. "I guess that's the oubliette," Ann said. "We call it the toilet." She left the room and shut the door behind her. "I'll stand by in case you get woozy."

Elizabeth would have been "woozy" even if she had not been ill, she thought. Everything in this Iowa was strange. Perhaps Joe and the sheriff were right. She must be raving; perhaps this was a fever dream. Perhaps soon she would awaken in her own bed, with Sukie at her side.

She looked for a pitcher of water to wash her hands.

"Fetch water for the washing basin," she called.

Ann opened the door. "We say please here, even when we're sick," she said. "And we flush the toilet when we're through."

When Ann pressed down the silver handle on the back, the chair made a loud noise, as water rushed into the chamber and out through a hole in the bottom. And Elizabeth had been sitting on this violent engine, oblivious to the danger! Yet Ann seemed calm, as if nothing unusual had happened.

Now she turned silver handles on the washing basin. "Do you know sinks with running water? Hot." She pointed at one handle. "And cold." She handed

Elizabeth a scented white block. "Do you know soap?"

"Of course I know soap!" said Elizabeth, beginning to wash her hands. "But the water is hot! It flowed from the spigot already hot!" She looked at Ann in dismay, with tears in her eyes. "Your manners and customs are foreign to me, but I am trying to understand." Her voice broke in spite of herself. "I am a nobleman's daughter. Do me the honor to treat me accordingly."

"How do noblemen's daughters get treated?" Ann pushed down a silver stick on the sink. "This is the plug."

Seeing the water swirl down a hole in the bottom of the basin, Elizabeth looked underneath for a pail, but found only a silver pipe that led into the wall. Perhaps the pail was in another chamber, below, and the servants emptied the waste.

Elizabeth looked into the mirror that hung above the sink and saw that Ann was staring at her.

"All of this really is new to you, isn't it? Where did you come from?" The cat was purring in Ann's arms. "And when? What year is this, Elizabeth?"

"Why, this is the year of our Lord, 1600," said Elizabeth. "Anybody knows the year. And I come from London, as I have told the others, time and again."

"Do you think I'm so dumb I'd believe such a silly story?" Ann asked. "1600?"

Elizabeth saw Ann's searching look in the mirror.

"Anybody knows that this is 1988," Ann went on. "And London is thousands of miles away, across the Atlantic Ocean."

"Do not toy with me," said Elizabeth with dignity, watching Ann for a smile or a gleam in her eye or any sign that she was joking or making fun. Then, unable to bear the thought that she might be altogether lost, in time as well as place, she splashed her face, as if to wash cobwebs from her mind.

She turned to Ann with the same imperial bearing she had seen the Queen use in troubled times. "I shall require a servant. Send me a maidservant to help me into bed. Or are you to be my maid?"

"We're fresh out of maids, Lizzie," said Ann with her nose in the air. "I'll help you because you're sick and crazy. But the Duke and Duchess had better pick you up pretty soon, or you'll have to learn to wait on yourself."

For supper, Kathy brought Elizabeth a bowl of chicken soup with dumplings floating in it that Ann called "wontons." Elizabeth ate two spoonfuls of the broth.

"These crackers will settle your stomach." Kathy pointed at a thin, white, salty biscuit on the tray. "And you need fluids to keep your fever down."

Elizabeth sipped a tumbler of a clear drink with bubbles rising in it, thinking it champagne. The bubbles prickled in her nose. "'Tis sweeter than wine," she said, sipping again.

"Soda pop," said Ann. "7-Up."

Elizabeth lay back in the featherbed, unable to eat more, and hugged Mariah to her breast. Kathy tucked the coverlet up around her ear, kissed her on the cheek, and turned the crank on the music box. Elizabeth heard Ann clatter down the stairs, followed by Kathy's lighter step. The cat glanced once at Elizabeth and bounded after them.

As the Summermusic played, Elizabeth thought of home. Whenever she was quiet, whenever her thoughts could stray where they might, she returned to Charington. In her imagination, she ran across the broad green lawn in front of the house, throwing the red ball for the spaniel Puck to chase, as Sukie watched from the stone portico.

She remembered the Twelfth Night parties her parents held every year at Christmastime. Elizabeth and her cousin Andrew would imitate their parents dancing a stately dance, while a quartet played music at the end of the room. The sweet strings sang, and dozens of women in dresses with great hoop skirts of silk or velvet, and men in doublets and brightly colored hose whirled about the great hall. A hundred candles flickered brilliant light that was reflected in the crystal drops of chandeliers. Sometimes the hot wax from the candles dripped on the ladies' wigs.

[39]

But although he was Elizabeth's own age, dancing had never interested Andrew. He kept stopping the dance to draw the miniature sword he wore at his side like his father's, just as Elizabeth would soon wear the small ruff and farthingale like her mother's.

"En garde!" Andrew had declared, and plunged his short sword at a nonexistent enemy.

Elizabeth might be kidnapped and ill, lying in a stranger's bed in a foreign country, but she could transport herself home in an instant of imagination. She saw Andrew now in her mind, as he had been last Twelfth Night. She saw him return his sword to its gold scabbard, saying, "Let's play tag! Better, let's play hide-and-seek!"

"Let's dance," Elizabeth had answered. "Or let's play dolls." But she knew that Andrew would not play dolls, and, if he danced, he would complain and act the fool until even Elizabeth would not enjoy the music and the elegance.

"Can't catch me!" she said, dodging behind a pillar.

The music played and the dancers danced, and Elizabeth ran out of the ballroom and down the long gallery where candles burned below the dark high portraits of her ancestors. She ran past the enormous tapestries with the minute stitches of a hundred artisans forming a hunting scene. She dodged round and round the carved oak furniture, as agile and athletic as any boy.

Panting for breath, but still far ahead, she hid in an alcove. When Andrew ran by, she jumped out and caught him by the waist. They fell, laughing, in a tangle on the carpet.

That is where Sukie found them. Elizabeth felt a hand on her shoulder, pulling her to her feet. "Ladies must act like ladies," Sukie admonished, sounding more imperious than any noblewoman. "You will spend the rest of the evening in your chamber, Miss Elizabeth. Perhaps with some thought, you'll learn to understand your place in the world."

Now, lying in her Iowa bed, Elizabeth felt so home-sick that Sukie's punishment seemed almost tender. But Sukie was far away. Longing for home, Elizabeth smiled to think how red Sukie's face had been on an-other night when once again Elizabeth had not known her place or stayed in it.

She had longed for some other playmates besides Andrew, especially playmates who were girls. She wished that Mother and Father would allow her to play with Nancy and Martha, the servant girls who were Elizabeth's age and lived straight at the top of the back stairs. Once she had crept up to their tiny room in the attic. But when the maidservants saw who had come through the door, they curtsied and hung their heads and looked at Elizabeth through their straggly hair, just as always.

Elizabeth had brought Mariah. "We could play

dolls," she said, holding out the doll with the beautiful porcelain face, and the lace nightdress that matched Elizabeth's own, and the blue glass eyes.

Nancy glanced at the pile of gray rags with stitched eyes and nose and mouth that lay tucked under the coarse blanket on her bed. Martha clutched a similar ragged heap to her heart. They bobbed a curtsy and said, "Yes, Miss, yes, Miss," in chorus.

Beginning to shiver in the servants' unheated room, Elizabeth sat on one of the rickety beds and covered her bare feet with her long nightdress.

Suddenly Sukie burst through the open doorway. "Back to your bed, Lady Elizabeth!" she said.

And all the way down the long stone stairs, Elizabeth heard Sukie scolding Nancy and Martha. "Good servants know their place," she heard. ". . . Daughter of a duke! . . . must never, never pretend to be her equal!"

But that was last year. Where were Nancy and Martha now, while Elizabeth lay aching in a strange bed in a strange land, with no mother or father, as well as no friend? Nancy and Martha might be sweeping the hearths or laying the fires or polishing the silver with their rough and reddened hands.

Where was Andrew this night, Andrew whom she had played with only a few days before? Why, Andrew would be in his own bed, behind his own green draperies, while Elizabeth lay in this who-knew-where of

Iowa, in a plain peasant's cottage, under a patchwork quilt.

Her music box had run down. Slowly she turned the little silver crank again and drifted off to sleep on the Summermusic's tinkling flow.

CHAPTER SIX

Ann's Doll

A LOUD, OBNOXIOUS BUZZ startled Elizabeth awake the next morning, as Ann lit the lamp and stumbled out of bed to stop the noise.

"What is it?" said Elizabeth.

"It's only the alarm clock." Ann rubbed her eyes.

Elizabeth remembered the deep, musical church bells that declared the time to everyone in London. "What o'clock is it?"

"The 'o'clock' is six A.M.," said Ann. "I have to get ready for school." The cat raised its head and peeped drowsily through half-closed eyes.

Elizabeth watched Ann pulling on clean rough clothes just like the ones she had worn yesterday. Ann made her bed with a few deft movements and tucked a red-haired doll under the quilt.

"What did your mother call your pantaloons and blouse?" Elizabeth asked.

"Jeans and sweatshirt, of course." Ann looked at Elizabeth with puzzlement in her eyes. "Are you still feverish and crazy? Don't you wear jeans in your country?"

"Only peasants wear such coarse cloth. In London, only beggars and apprentices."

"Oh, don't start in on that duke's daughter stuff again!" Ann said. "I'm not crazy about outfitting you in my clothes anyway."

"What have I said to offend you? I but spoke the truth."

"Don't act so stuck-up, Miss Smartypants. You'll have to live the way we — " Ann stopped her angry outburst when Kathy's footsteps sounded on the stairs.

"'Morning, girls." Kathy smiled and embraced her daughter just as Elizabeth's nurse Sukie greeted her every morning. Kathy was wearing a suit of fine woolen today, Elizabeth noticed, and a bright red silk blouse. She was not dressed for pigs. "I made blueberry pancakes this morning," Kathy went on. "Come and get 'em while they're hot."

Here was another amazement, Elizabeth thought, as Kathy kissed her cheek. A mother who arose with her child in the chill morning and cooked the breakfast herself before the sun came up, a mother who did the work of a nurse and cook.

Elizabeth thought of her meager one-hour visit with her own mother every morning and her hour's appointment for studies with her father in the afternoon. Her visits with her parents flew. The rest of the day she spent with Mother's maid, learning fancy stitchery, or with the music master, learning to play the lute, or studying languages, painting, and history with her tutor. Although most people did not, Father and the Queen thought the education of women important.

Now Kathy was embracing Elizabeth. "How are you feeling today?"

Elizabeth thought of her illness for the first time. "Miraculously better, as if the Queen herself had blessed me."

Kathy laughed. "Penicillin's the blessing queen around here. Also the miracle. That shot the doctor gave you in your leg yesterday. Remember? And the tablets the doctor sent home with you." Kathy felt Elizabeth's forehead with her palm. "Are you up to eating pancakes? Ann, lend her your robe and come to breakfast."

Then Kathy was gone.

Ann tossed a long gown onto the floor between the beds. "My bathrobe, Miss Queen of Sheba."

Elizabeth put her music box under the pillow and dragged herself out of bed. "Oh, I am woozy yet." She picked up the robe and looked at it with disgust. It was not quilted rose satin like her own, but something fuzzy and pink and much too garish.

Ann sat on her bed and watched Elizabeth struggle with the armholes and sleeves of the robe, but she did not move to help. "Don't you even know how to get dressed?" she asked.

"Sukie has always helped me," Elizabeth said.

"Helped you dress? At your age?" Ann snorted in obvious scorn.

Feeling embarrassed about her awkwardness with Ann's judging eyes upon her, Elizabeth turned her back. She had never thought about dressing herself. Everyone she knew dressed with the help of servants. The maid laced up Mother's corset and dropped her full-skirted gown over her shoulders and brushed her hair and set her wig upon her head. The valet laid out Father's clothes and buttoned his waistcoat; often there were twenty buttons to pull through twenty loops. Then the valet trimmed and combed father's beard and moustache and straightened the seams of his hose.

Elizabeth had never thought before that she might like to fend for herself, rather than wait for Sukie, who took her time about everything. Sometimes she made Elizabeth wait on purpose, to feel her power. Elizabeth imagined herself dressing alone before anyone else awoke, even before the fires were stoked up on the hearths, and walking with Puck to the brook where the village children played among the cattails.

Sukie said that the grass was wet with dew in the morning. "You mustn't go out until the dew dries," she always warned. "You'll take a chill from damp feet. You'll spoil your pretty slippers."

You'll this and you'll that, Elizabeth thought now as she looked for hooks to close the front of the robe. What would it be like to play without the warnings and watchings of servants? To take off her shoes in the morning chill, to run barefoot in the dew, leaving dark footprints across the silvery green? To throw a ball for Puck without Sukie's admonishments about acting like a lady? To pick up a frog in her bare hand?

But where were the hooks for this robe? She turned back to face Ann, who was sitting on her hands, smiling smugly.

"Please help me," Elizabeth begged. "I am sorry that I hurt your feelings."

Her apology to an underling stuck in Elizabeth's throat, but Ann did not notice. "Just tie the belt around your waist," she said.

Elizabeth found the sash that trailed behind her like a tail, and tied it in the front.

"I shall try to live as you do," she said, "until the ransom has been paid and you return me to my parents."

An exasperated cry arose from Ann's throat. "You are too much!" she yelled as she slammed out of the room. Elizabeth heard her clatter down the stairs and howl, "That stuckup kid still thinks we kidnapped her! She actually thinks we want her!"

Elizabeth sat down heavily and stared across at Ann's neatly made bed. She smoothed her own feather-erbed, plumped the pillow as Sukie always did, and struggled to pull the quilt up over the pillow. The covers lay in heavy wrinkles and hung crooked and uneven. Elizabeth didn't care. Bedmaking was servants' work anyway.

She stroked Mariah's chestnut hair. Perhaps these McCormicks were peasants, vulgar and poor. But they owned treasures no nobleman in England had ever imagined. And what they had they were sharing with her. She tried again to pull the bed linen smooth and straightened the quilt until it was almost as neat as Ann's. Servants' work was not as easy as they made it look.

She took the coarse doll from under Ann's quilt. Its body was stuffed cloth, like Mariah's, but so was its head. It had no delicate porcelain face with exquisitely formed lips, no chestnut ringlets or claret velvet dress.

Its round face was blank, except for stitched black eyes, a smiling mouth, and a stitched triangle for a nose. A wreath of clipped red yarn for hair encircled its face. It wore a blue dress covered by a white apron, and red-and-white striped hose. The shoes were not handmade of kidskin, like Mariah's, but merely black extensions of the doll's cloth legs.

A worn rag doll, then. Elizabeth covered it up again so neatly Ann would never know that anyone had

touched it. A rag doll, cleaner and brighter but otherwise not much better than the heaps of rags she had
seen Martha the scullery maid clasping to her heart.

A rag doll – but a doll.

And Ann, perhaps, a playmate.

CHAPTER SEVEN

The Test

"**D**ON'T FORGET YOUR BACKPACK," Kathy called. Ann rushed back into the kitchen, slung the strap of a bright red bag over her shoulder, and rushed out the door again.

Through the front window, Elizabeth watched her climb steps into a long yellow carriage, with children at every window and black letters on the side that spelled, "Blackhawk County Schools." Even with the house closed up against the morning chill, Elizabeth could hear the horrifying roar as the carriage pulled away.

She turned to Kathy, who was watching her. "What power makes your carriages go, without horses and oxen? What is the terrible smoke that billows from the rear?"

Kathy sat down in a wooden chair and pulled Elizabeth near. "That's the school bus. An engine in the front makes it go." Kathy brushed Elizabeth's hair back with her hand. "It's true, isn't it? You've never seen an engine before?"

"We have engines in London." Kathy seemed to think that London was behind the times. "Our engines run on the power of the Thames."

Elizabeth remembered the time she had boosted herself up onto a window ledge in one of the shops that lined London Bridge. She had leaned far out to spit into the swirling water below.

Sukie's hands had trembled as she hauled Elizabeth back inside. "Fall in that river, and you're gone forever," Sukie had said. "That river is a thief."

But the Thames was also generous. "I suppose you've heard of our wonderful new water system," Elizabeth said to Kathy. "Father says 'tis one of the modern wonders of the world. The river powers the pumps that carry water through pipes to all the city. Father says 'tis only the newest of the inventions that make London the most modern city in Europe."

Kathy stared at Elizabeth. "After you went to bed last night," she said, "I read a little about Elizabethan London, to refresh my memory. How in the world do you know about the London waterworks?" She shook her head. "You couldn't possibly have lived in 1600."

She took Elizabeth's hand. "Do you hear that noise from the utility room?" She led Elizabeth into a small room near the back door, where she opened a low cupboard and pointed inside at a black box that whirred and clicked and clacked. "That's our water pump," she said, her voice all matter-of-fact now. "But it isn't powered by water like London's."

Kathy flipped a short silver stick; the box fell quiet. She flipped the stick again; the box instantly whirred and clicked and clacked. "Now it's pumping water out of the well again."

"But how?" said Elizabeth.

"Electricity," said Kathy. "The school bus has a bigger engine that runs on gasoline."

Electricity. Gasoline. These foreign words might be spells, Elizabeth thought.

"You flip the switch now," said Kathy, "but keep your fingers away from the wheel and belt."

With a pounding heart, Elizabeth pushed the silver switch and quickly pulled her hand away. The box fell quiet once more. She flipped the switch back again. The box whirred and chugged.

"The lights work on electricity too. Here's the switch over here." Kathy reached toward a white rectangle on the wall beside the door, and shifted a squared-off knob in the middle. Something snuffed the candle in the globe overhead. The room instantly darkened, lit dimly by only the kitchen windows.

"Is there a mechanical snuffer inside the wall and ceiling somehow?"

"No. The light is not a candle. It works on electricity, just like the stove in the kitchen and Annie's alarm clock."

But it must be a candle, or a torch, or an oil lamp. Or magic, Elizabeth thought, as the fear rose in her breast.

Kathy pressed the switch again, and the candle flared once more. It had relit itself somehow! "Now you do it."

Elizabeth blessed herself, with a trembling hand. Then she pressed the switch, touching it only for a moment and then pulling her hand away. Quicker than abracadabra, she had banished light. And the switch did not feel magical, but seemed to be an ordinary physical object. She flipped it again. The candle flared as bright as ever. Again darkness. Light again. Darkness. Light.

Elizabeth smiled as she played with the light switch. "I can bring light out of darkness," she exclaimed. "I can snuff a candle without touching it, without making any smoke, without knowing any spells."

Kathy laughed and hugged Elizabeth.

"I don't understand it. It is too much for me to comprehend," said Elizabeth. "Do you say spells? The Archbishop says that magic spells are evil."

"I don't quite understand it myself," said Kathy. She held Elizabeth's shoulders and looked intently at her face. "It isn't magic, though, but a power in nature that we've learned to control. We would feel wonder, too, if we weren't so accustomed to this power."

This kindness, added to mystery, piled upon strangeness, was more than Elizabeth could bear. If Kathy had beaten her and starved her, like an ordinary kidnapper, she could have stood the pain and hunger. But Kathy's kindness brought memories of Sukie and Mother, and such memories made her cry, here in Iowa.

"I want to go home," Elizabeth said. "I fear the sickness will take my mother. My father will worry about me."

Kathy put her arms around her. "Oh, my dear," she said. "We're trying to find your people. If only your confusion would pass. When your memory clears, you can tell the sheriff who you are."

"Memory! I remember everything!" said Elizabeth. "What I am is the daughter of a duke in Queen Elizabeth's court. Why do you doubt me?"

"Coincidental as it may seem, Elizabeth, I'm a historian. I've studied English history since I was a girl. There was indeed a Michael, Duke of Umberland, in the Elizabethan court. But that was almost four hundred years ago!" Kathy held Elizabeth's face gently in her hands as they searched one another's eyes.

"If what you say were true," said Elizabeth uncertainly, "then you could tell me the future. Will my mother die?"

"I haven't had time to read much, but I did find that the Duchess of Umberland was alive in 1605. But of course, she couldn't be your mother."

"Why do you doubt me?"

"I'm a scholar. I feel ridiculous discussing time travel as if it were possible," Kathy went on as quietly as if she were talking to herself. "But if it will help you feel better, I'll listen to your stories."

"I know nothing of time travel. I tell you no stories, only the truth. 'Tis ridiculous to speak of my lifetime as if it were long ago!"

"Well, then, let's see what you know."

"What shall I say?"

"Who was Philip the Second?"

"The King of Spain. He courted the Queen and wished to marry her. Failing that, he sent an Armada of ships against us. Francis Drake and John Hawkins destroyed them, but we are still at war." Elizabeth caught her breath and watched Kathy for signs of doubt. "Why do you ask such an easy question? Even the simpletons in London know about the war and the King of Spain."

"Well, you passed the easy test," said Kathy. "Here's a harder one. Tell me what you know about Robert Dudley."

"He was the Earl of Leicester, the Queen's favorite, who died before I was born. 'Tis whispered that the Queen loved him."

"Someone has coached you well."

"Coached me! No one need coach me about the gossip I hear every day, at every lawn party and every court ball!"

Kathy smiled wryly and went on with the quiz. "Who was Essex?"

"Essex is Robert Devereux. Given to bullheaded will, my father says." Elizabeth smiled, remembering her father's charming, dangerous friend. "He always calls me 'Poppet.' I told him that I am too old for such childish names – I shall soon be wearing a ruff like Mother's – but he goes on just the same as when I crept on hands and knees!"

"There you have it wrong, Elizabeth. Essex was a gadfly, surely too dangerous for Umberland to embrace as a friend in his own home."

"Some say that unless Essex curbs his defiance of the Queen, he will end by losing his head. But Father says that friends are true, even when danger looms." Elizabeth looked defiantly at Kathy. "I keep my ears open and my mouth closed. People often say dangerous things in my presence, thinking me too ignorant to understand. I daresay that I know things your historians do not imagine."

"You really seem to believe what you're telling me," said Kathy, staring, as if Elizabeth were one of those impossible Chinese puzzles carved in ivory like the one Father had given Mother for a gift.

"Of course I believe it! These people are my friends."

Kathy sighed. "You are a most determined little girl," she said. "All right then. The Queen. She made herself so grand and unapproachable, she hardly seems flesh and blood when you read about her, let alone feminine flesh and blood. Tell me about the Queen."

Elizabeth smiled. "You sound as curious as one of the stablemen who gossip while they trim the horses' hooves."

"Yes, I suppose I do. I've buried myself so long in libraries, my hair is full of dust. See here?" Kathy stroked the streaks of gray at her temples. "I've always longed to be a mouse at Elizabeth's court, and not just a scholar reading ancient documents. What do you suppose the Queen was like? What color was her hair, I wonder, under those magnificent red wigs?"

"'Tis gray and wispy," said Elizabeth. "But only her ladies-in-waiting and I know. And now you." She shook her finger at Kathy. "You mustn't tell. 'Tis a state secret, the Queen says, that she is old. I have never even told Mother."

"Her grandeur was her only protection," said Kathy.

What if Kathy told the secrets Elizabeth had revealed — that Father loved his friend Essex, that the Queen was old? But Iowa was so distant, surely Kathy could never tell a Spanish spy.

Memories of home came crowding in again on Elizabeth, like so many thunderclouds blown by the wind. "Home seems so far away," she said, tears coursing down her cheeks.

"Yes, so it seems to be," said Kathy. "You make the past seem real. These personal details are so convincing, you almost draw me into your delusions." She stroked Elizabeth's hair. "Of course, you can't have traveled through time. Such things don't happen, except in stories."

"I swear upon my father's head and my mother's soul, 'tis true! 'Tis true!"

And the Lady Elizabeth bent down on one knee to kiss the ring of the peasant. She looked into Kathy's plain round face, a face like Sukie's, and she kissed the ring again. "I beg of you," she said. "Take me home!"

CHAPTER EIGHT

The False Queen

KATHY SAT DOWN in a chair and pulled Elizabeth into her lap, hugging her tight and caressing her head, as Sukie did when Elizabeth was troubled.

"Your illness has made you imagine strange things," said Kathy. "I don't understand your confusion any better than you do. But trust me on one thing. We didn't kidnap you. I swear."

Looking back into her gray eyes, Elizabeth believed her.

"I think you should stay in bed another day, even though you feel better," said Kathy. "Here are some books and magazines for you to read while I'm at work. Joe will carry the TV set up to your room, and he'll make lunch for you."

How strange to find books in a peasant's house. "I thought you worked in the byre."

"I do sometimes," said Kathy, "when Joe needs help in the barn and I happen to be handy." She stood up and tucked some papers she had been reading at the table into a leather satchel. "Most days, though, I'm at the university in Cedar Falls. I teach history there. That's why I'm dressed so spiffy now."

She took Elizabeth's hand and picked up the stack of books. "Come on. I'll tuck you in."

Elizabeth was as dumfounded as she would have been had a dog stood on its hind legs and declared in English that it taught history at Oxford. Yesterday, unless Elizabeth was dreaming, Kathy had been a swineherd, wearing men's pantaloons. Today she said she taught at university. And the physician. That Shanasha person – the doctor herself had been a woman!

"In England," said Elizabeth, "only gentlemen may enroll at university. And certainly gentlemen would not listen to a female tutor."

"Elizabeth, you're so old-fashioned. That attitude is really outdated now. The English universities have accepted women students for some time." Kathy plumped Elizabeth's pillow, smoothed her sheets, and helped her into bed. "Do you read a lot of books about the olden days?"

"Sometimes. Father and I have been reading Plutarch's *Lives*."

"Oh, I've read those heroic biographies too. You have a children's edition in English?"

"We read the same Plutarch everybody else reads.

The Greek one," said Elizabeth, annoyed that Kathy would condescend to her. "And the Queen teaches me the modern languages every Tuesday afternoon. I already speak French quite well, she says, and now we're learning Spanish. 'Tis a good thing for a monarch, the Queen says, to understand the language her enemies speak."

Elizabeth shifted the pillow under her head. "Once the Queen overheard the Spanish ambassador's aide whispering behind his hand." She showed Kathy how sneaky the man had looked. "'This little bewigged and black-toothed bitch shouldn't be hard to trick,' he said in Spanish. He didn't know that the Queen speaks eight languages."

Elizabeth remembered the Queen's laughter when she told the story of that state meeting with the Spanish King's ambassador. "She wanted to growl and bark and bite his hand with her black teeth, she told me. Instead she kept her Spanish a secret, hoping to hear what the trick might be."

So vivid were her memories that Elizabeth had forgotten for an instant where she was. She glanced at Kathy, whose face was screwed up. She looked as puzzled as Elizabeth felt. "What is it?" Elizabeth asked.

"How do you know how many languages Queen Elizabeth the First could speak?" Kathy asked in a very quiet voice. "How do you know about her black teeth? Who has taught you such detailed personal history?"

"Queen Elizabeth the Only," said Elizabeth. "Why wouldn't I know she has black teeth? I dine with her every Tuesday afternoon! Don't eat too many jam tarts, she always tells me, or my teeth will look like hers."

Kathy rubbed her eyes, as if she were overcome by a headache. "We'll talk some more about this when I come home from work." She dropped a booklet in Elizabeth's lap. "In the meantime, if you can read Plutarch in Greek, *Time* magazine won't tax your mind too much." She smiled. "While Ann and I are gone, Prissy will keep you company."

Elizabeth looked around for a servant.

"The cat." Kathy picked up the tabbycat that was weaving in and out between her feet and put it on the foot of the bed.

· Elizabeth watched her walk away in slippers with strange, grotesquely high heels that clattered on the stairs. "Joe's in the barn, if you need anything," Kathy called. "See you later, kiddo."

Elizabeth heard the back door slam. A moment later, she heard the red coach with the – what sort of engine had Kathy called it? A gasoline engine. She looked out and saw the carriage roar away under the window. Kathy herself was driving.

I am alone in the house, Elizabeth thought. Now I can escape! But where would she go? She remembered the fields that stretched away forever in the distance. The road had led straight to nowhere, to a strange town called Cedar Falls with wide paved streets between rows of peculiar cottages.

Nowhere had she smelled the Thames. The river here was a narrow one, nothing like the great waterway of London that flowed so rapidly under bridges that boaters must beware for their lives. She had heard neither the bells nor the street merchants' chants that made the London streets an unceasing commotion. Rather than starve on the road to nowhere, she would stay in this haven until she could learn the way from Iowa to London.

Elizabeth picked up the pamphlet Kathy had left on her lap. What had she called it? A magazine. Big letters said TIME across the top, above a portrait of two women that was more exact and true-to-life than any painting she had ever seen. The elder woman wore a plain blue coat and a matching blue hat. The young woman beside her was not so ordinary. She was blond and very pretty, and her clothes looked "spiffy."

Then Elizabeth noticed the words under the picture: "Great Britain's Queen Elizabeth II and Princess Diana."

Elizabeth gasped. This woman, in her plain garb, a queen? Elizabeth thought of her own dear Queen, dressed for court in a satin gown encrusted with pearls and rubies, wearing a splendid red wig, her head framed in a great lace collar. The Queen's gown, afloat on hoops that kept everyone at a distance, always reminded Elizabeth of a sailing ship. Everyone who spoke to the Queen did so on his knees. And she had forbidden the pamphleteers to print any portraits without her permission.

But then Elizabeth recalled the Queen in her private chambers on Tuesday afternoons, teaching her young friend chess. She always wore a simply cut, undecorated woolen gown, often gray or lavender, loose at the waist. Without her regal manner and her great-skirted costume, the Queen seemed to have shrunk. Her body looked as frail as any common grandmother's.

But the magazine called this blue-coated woman "Great Britain's Queen Elizabeth II." There was but one Queen Elizabeth, and she had been crowned in 1558. Most people could not remember the time before Queen Elizabeth, Gloriana, had reigned.

How dare this upstart masquerade as the Queen's successor! How dare the pamphleteers print such a picture! The whole world had gone mad.

And then Elizabeth looked at the date of the magazine. October 10. That was correct; Sukie had told her the date yesterday morning.

But the year! Just as Ann had said, the year on the pamphlet was 1988.

CHAPTER NINE

The Road to Nowhere

INSIDE *TIME MAGAZINE*, Elizabeth quickly found a story about the false queen. Under another portrait of the woman in the plain blue coat were the words, "Queen Elizabeth prepares to fly to Canada." She laughed for the first time since she had come to Iowa, imagining the spectacle of a queen flapping her arms and soaring like a bird.

She paged through the rest of the magazine from front cover to back. The stories were all as fantastic as the one about the false queen. They were as fantastic as the *Odyssey*, the Greek tale she and Father had read last year, about a sailor who landed on an enchanted island where a sorceress changed sailors into pigs. Elizabeth thought with a smile that perhaps all the pigs in this Iowa byre had once been sailors.

The magazine was full of imaginary places like Canada and Mexico. Many stories and portraits were shocking. Elizabeth found a picture of ladies lying in the sun beside the ocean with their arms and legs and even other parts of their bodies exposed for everyone to see. Similarly naked men and women were passing by without a blink, as if nothing were unusual. Elizabeth blushed and turned the page.

There was a wild man, with a ring in his nose and his hair painted green. He was a minstrel playing a strange musical instrument, something like a mandolin, but his face and body were contorted as if he were in a rage. What sort of music could this be?

She turned the crank of her music box and held the cool carved wood to her cheek. With her forefinger, she caressed Mariah's face, stroking the porcelain lips and eyes. These things transported her home again, away from this madhouse of Iowa. And what of her mother? The servants had whispered that her mother would die without medicine. Elizabeth imagined her dead, with the sheet pulled over her face and the candles lit while the chaplain read prayers and Father wept.

She covered her eyes and listened to the Summer-music, thinking that Sukie would be looking high and low through the house for her girl, weeping and calling. As Elizabeth began to weep herself, she turned again to the magazine, trying to distract her thoughts in a story called "Science." The caption said, "How has America benefited from sending men to the moon?"

Enough nonsense! This barbaric place, with its naked ladies on the beach, its wild minstrels, and its fantastic stories was no place for the daughter of a duke of the realm. She must escape the kidnappers, find a way out of Iowa, and go home to nurse her mother.

She felt woozy as she sat up on the side of the bed, but she knew that she must go now, while Joe was working and Kathy and Ann were away. She must escape before Joe came to the house to make the lunch and carry up the TV, whatever that might be. She dressed as quickly as she could in Ann's strange clothes, the sweatshirt and jeans, the socks and pink sneakers. She stopped only a moment to try the amazing metal fastener that Ann had called a zipper. Prissy sat on her haunches and watched.

In the closet, Elizabeth found another backpack like the one Ann had taken to school. She tucked Mariah and her music box inside and then hurried downstairs to the big white box in the kitchen where she had seen Kathy store the food. Everything inside was cold! She put several apples in her backpack; surely apples would be the same food anywhere.

She found some paper boxes labeled "Cranberry Juice." Who could say what cranberries were? But

Elizabeth liked berries of all kinds at home in London, especially those wild strawberries the urchins sold on the streets in spring. She would certainly not eat the package of sausages marked "hot dogs," out of respect for Puck. But the meat in a glass jar labeled "dried beef" looked blessedly familiar.

She swallowed the day's second dose of penicillin as Kathy had told her to do, and put the bottle in the pouch pocket of her sweatshirt. Although she still felt ill, she was stronger than she had been only yesterday. Perhaps this medicine really did cure an ague like her mother's, which had resisted the potions of even the Queen's own lordly physician. What a blessing it would be to take this medicine to her mother. The medicine! Why had she not thought of that before?

She went out the front door, on the side of the house away from the barn, so Joe couldn't see her go, and looked up and down the road that ran perfectly straight between the fields and past the house. It was a dirt road, not paved with cobblestones like the broad main streets of London, but wider and smoother than any of the country tracks Elizabeth had ever seen.

Which way to go? One way looked the same as the other. Elizabeth shut her eyes, turned around and around, and then followed the path her eyes showed her when she opened them again.

As she walked, she looked across the harvested corn with amazement, for the land was flat, stretching miles away to the horizon, and the fields were huge, big enough to grow food for whole cities, and not just a patch for the farmer's family. Flocks of blackbirds wheeled in the sky and alighted suddenly by unanimous decision to glean the seeds the harvesters had missed. The day was as blue and cool as the finest day in England.

She walked steadily, occasionally winding her music box for company, and often looking back to see how far she had come from Ann's house. Once she saw a bird singing on a post, red-breasted like the robins at home, but bigger and more rangy. Far down the road, she saw something approaching, so far away she could discern only movement, not its shape. She began to plan what she would say to strangers. As little as possible, she was sure, a nod and hello and little smile. She mustn't arouse suspicion or let a stranger hear the way she talked.

But the stranger was only a hound with a red collar on his neck. He nuzzled her hand when she held it out and then followed along behind her, as if he didn't care where he went so long as he had company.

Hearing a roar overhead, she looked up. Higher than any hawk, a silver bird moved straight through the heavens, without even flapping its wings. A puffy white tail followed it halfway across the sky. What manner of bird could fly so straight without flapping its wings?

At last, when she looked back, she saw that the

farmhouse was tiny in the distance. But her steps were slowing and her legs were wobbly. She sat down in the dusty grass along the side of the road to rest and eat an apple. It was much larger than any apple she had ever seen, and it tasted good, but her stomach was queasy and she couldn't eat much. The dog nosed her backpack and licked her cheek.

In the distance, a cloud of dust approached with a white carriage leading it. She felt too ill to run, and looking around, she saw no place to hide, only the shallow grass-filled ditch and the shorn field where even blackbirds were plain to see. She would wave at the driver as he passed. Perhaps he would not be curious.

The driver waved back. Elizabeth gasped when she saw who he was and read the word "Sheriff" on the door of his carriage. Red lights flashed in the back. As Elizabeth held her breath, the car slowed, came to a stop, and began to back up. Her heart pounded. The man would catch her, but she was too ill to run away.

As the dog trotted away up the road, Sheriff Cox stepped out of the car with a big smile on his face. "I'm glad you were heading my way, Elizabeth," he said. "I want to talk with you some more. Come along with me back to Joe's. I heard a little something about your folks."

News of her parents! Elizabeth jumped into the car and traveled back to the McCormicks' farm with a glad heart.

CHAPTER TEN

A Dire Prophecy

"KEEP ME WAITING no longer, I beg of you," Elizabeth implored. "Mother and Father. You have found them?"

Before the Sheriff could reply, Joe reached across the table and took Elizabeth's hand. She glanced at him and squeezed, grateful once again that this smiling, golden man had not been angry when Sheriff Cox returned her to the farm.

As he had driven Elizabeth back to the McCormicks' place, Sheriff Cox told Elizabeth all the wrong paths he had followed and all the false information he had gathered, but he reported nothing of her parents.

"Look who I found half a mile up the road," the

sheriff had said when Joe heard his name called and stepped out of the barn.

"Well, of course!" Joe had reached down and scooped Elizabeth up in his arms. "I wouldn't give a bent nail for someone who wouldn't try to escape from a pinch." He gave Elizabeth a pat. "Sorry I've neglected you. I thought you'd be sleeping, not feeling well enough for a morning stroll."

Now the three of them were sitting at the kitchen table, the two men calmly sipping coffee while Elizabeth nearly burst with excitement.

"Tell us about it, Ned," said Joe, stirring a spoon around his coffee cup with his free hand. "But Elizabeth can't wait for all the preliminary details. Have you found her folks?"

"No, not exactly."

Elizabeth slumped, the disappointment heavy on her head.

"Well, what exactly have you found," said Joe. "Elizabeth and I can't stand all this hemming and hawing."

"We do have some leads," said the sheriff. "We called the British consulate in Chicago to find out about this here Michael and Margaret, Duke and Duchess of Umberland." He consulted his notepad. "And Charington House, London."

"What did they say?" Elizabeth fairly screamed.

"Well, sir, there was a House of Umberland up until

the eighteenth century. That's when the consulate woman said the family line petered out."

"Petered out? Eighteenth century?" said Elizabeth.

"Yes. You know. No heirs. No children to inherit the dukedom."

Elizabeth laughed without feeling mirth. "Why do you bait me so? 'Tis but the beginning of the seventeenth century now. I do not believe your fantastic stories about history." She shook her head, bewildered by the idea that her family might have gone out of existence a hundred years or so after she was born.

"What about Michael and Margaret, Elizabeth's parents?" asked Joe.

"That's the strange part," said Ned Cox. "There never was a Michael and Margaret in the Umberland line after 1625, when they both died of the plague."

Elizabeth gasped. "What nonsense are you talking?" This sheriff was a fool. "Father was well but yesterday morning. And my mother's disease is not the plague; all the physicians agreed."

Elizabeth gathered courage as she talked. "I was born in 1591, and I am now but nine years old." The 1988 date on the *Time* magazine flitted through her mind and reminded her that something strange had happened not only in a magazine entitled *Time*, but to time itself. "How is it that you and Kathy speak as if 1625 were in the past? I cannot understand it."

"Oh, my dear," said Joe, looking as bewildered as

Elizabeth felt. "Fevers do strange things to our sense. What I can't figure out, though, is how you learned all this stuff about the past in the first place. And where you came by that beautiful costume you were wearing the first time I saw you, dressed like a princess, in the pigpen." He reached out to her with both big hands.

Elizabeth clasped Joe's hands in her own, thinking of her parents' death from the plague, and swallowed back the tears that welled in her throat. The sheriff's nonsense seemed more and more real in her imagination, but she stuffed down her anxiety and turned to him in anger. "I do not believe you. But tell me the rest of what you have learned."

"That's about it," said Ned Cox. "There was a Charington House, but there isn't anymore. Burned to the ground in 1607."

"More nonsense!" Elizabeth blustered. "The year is 1600. And Charington still stands where it has always stood, among the great houses of the other courtiers. And what of me? What have you heard of me?"

"Not a word. But we're still trying. You could help us if you would tell us what you know."

"What I know is my mother and father and the house I have lived in all my life! I know them very well, indeed. What more can I tell you to lead you to my family?" Elizabeth was growing angrier with every sentence the sheriff uttered. How could this oaf condescend to her?

"What we really need to know, Elizabeth, is how you came to be traveling in Iowa. Who brought you here?"

"How many times must I tell you?" Elizabeth snapped, out of patience at last. "I came here on a zephyr or a moonbeam! When last I looked about me, Sukie was tucking me into bed and pulling the curtains while servant girls whispered in the room beyond. The next thing I knew, I was standing in Master McCormick's pig barn!"

Unable to say any more, Elizabeth hid her face in her hands, trembling uncontrollably. Joe moved his chair close to hers and put his arm around her shoulders without speaking.

When she had wept out all the tears that were in her, he said, "You're tuckered out from the hard morning you've had, and you're still sick. I'll carry you up to bed." As they climbed the stairs, he went on. "Remember that you'll always have a place with the McCormicks until we work this mess out together. Things might look a little brighter when you wake up."

Elizabeth lay huddled under the blankets for a long time, hearing over and over the sheriff's bleak report. What he seemed to regard as history was, for her, dire prophecy. There never was a Michael and Margaret, Sheriff Cox had said, after 1625, when they both died of the plague.

Until her mother's illness, death had seemed a disaster that happened only to other people. Now Ned Cox was telling her he knew the very year of her parents' death, and the cause. Elizabeth buried her face in Mariah's velvet dress and wept until she fell asleep.

CHAPTER ELEVEN

A Clouded Crystal Ball

FITFUL DREAMS DISTURBED Elizabeth's sleep all afternoon. When at last she opened her eyes, she saw Ann standing in a pool of dazzling sunlight beside her bed, looking at her gravely.

"I am glad you have come back," said Elizabeth.

"I'm sorry I was so cross this morning," Ann said. "Who did you say you were?"

"I was and am yet Lady Elizabeth, daughter of the Duke and Duchess of Umberland," she said, for what seemed like the hundredth time.

"Where do you live?" Ann's manner was intense, as if she could not wait for answers. "And what's the name of your house? And your parents' names?"

"Most of the year, we live in London, at Charington. In summer, and when the plague is raging, we go to the country. And my parents are Michael and Margaret." Elizabeth sighed. These fools still did not believe her. "Why are you asking me these questions again?"

"Mom helped me find the right history books in the study before I left for school this morning." Ann visibly curbed her excitement. "I still don't know whether to believe you, but you can help me check out your story if you want to. We can prove it, one way or the other."

"Anything to find my parents again. But why does everyone here insist upon talking about history? My parents were alive one day ago, in the year of our Lord, 1600."

Elizabeth sat up with an effort. "The sheriff talks of the eighteenth century as if it were long ago. That pamphlet bears the date 1988." She gestured in despair at the *Time* magazine she had thrown across the room in confusion. "And now you speak of finding me in histories. 'Tis too fantastic."

"I know." Ann's voice was softer. "But this year really is 1988. Cross my heart and hope to die, stick a needle in my eye." She drew an "X" on her chest with her finger. "You swear, too."

"'Sblood!" Elizabeth touched her forehead, her chest, and each shoulder with the tips of her fingers. "Cross my heart and hope to die."

"If you're honest, we'll find you in the books." Ann held her robe for Elizabeth. "Are you well enough to go downstairs to the study?"

"Yes. And you will see I am honest." Elizabeth would humor Ann and her talk of histories. It was nice to have her company, even though she spoke such foolishness, and they might stumble on a clue to the way home from Iowa.

"Bring your doll," said Ann, snatching her rag doll from under the quilt. She led the way downstairs, through a hallway off the kitchen, to the study. She blustered into the room, just as she did everything, chattering. "Here are the books, on Mom's desk."

She tucked her doll high up under her arm and picked up several volumes from the stacks of books piled amid papers and beach stones and feathers on one of the two large desks. "That's Dad's desk over there," she said, settling down against the puffed cushions of a flowered sofa that was arranged with two big, soft chairs before a broad stone fireplace.

She propped the doll against a pillow embroidered with stags and leaves. "Come on in." Ann looked up and beckoned to Elizabeth. "We can sit together on the couch."

But Elizabeth stood in the doorway with Mariah in her arm, looking with amazement at the walls lined from floor to ceiling with books. "Can you read?" Elizabeth asked. Although she knew Ann attended school, she was shocked that these peasants could afford a library that rivaled Father's own, and still amazed that they could even read at all. Father said that before Mr. Caxton brought the printing press to England, books had been copied by hand; even now, they were very expensive.

"Of course I can read. Can't you?" Not waiting for an answer, Ann pointed at the wall. "Those are Mom's books, and these are Dad's over here – his are mostly about plants and animals and money and business."

Ann walked to the far end of the room. "These are mine." Taking a book down, she held up her doll. "Raggedy Ann was born in this story about her. You can read it if you want to." She put the book back in its place and searched until she found another. "Here's the one for you – *A Wrinkle in Time*. The kids in this one are lost in space and time."

Ann went back to the sofa and beckoned again. "Come on."

Elizabeth did not answer. She was staring at a box that stood on a table beside the fireplace. Inside the box, flickering images of tiny human beings danced. A child no bigger than Elizabeth's hand was coaxing a shepherd dog like those that herded sheep and kept the wolves away from the flocks on the English moors.

"Oh, that's only the TV. You must have TV in England," said Ann.

The boy in the box was saying, "Come on, Lassie. Come." Elizabeth obeyed his command, mesmerized. She walked across the room toward Ann, her arm outstretched, to touch the boy and the dog with her pointed finger. Her manicured fingernail struck the hard surface of the box, and the boy and the dog ran across the moor, just as if Elizabeth did not exist and had not this moment struck them without meaning to. Jolly music arose from the box while the boy and the dog played. It was as if a sorcerer had breathed life into a perfectly natural painting and hidden elfin musicians behind the canvas.

"Haven't you ever seen TV?"

Elizabeth was speechless with wonder. She looked at the back of the box, but found only a tangle of wires and a grille. When she looked again at the moving picture, the boy and his dog had disappeared, and the music was gone. Now another boy sat eating at a table, while an invisible man talked about something he called "cornflakes."

"If it distracts you," said Ann, dismissing the magic as if it were nothing, "let's turn it off for now." She touched a small knob at the side. With a click, the boy and his bowl of porridge disappeared. The front of the box was no longer brightly lit, but gray and blank and lifeless.

"It's only TV," said Ann, as if repeating the word could explain the wonderful box.

[82]

"What happened to the tiny boy and the tiny dog? Where did they go when you touched the knob?"

"I don't know. I guess they went into the air." Ann didn't seem worried or even curious. "It works on electricity, but I don't understand how."

Electricity again. More magic spells. Feeling as if she were a walking dreamer, Elizabeth sat down beside Ann and settled Mariah on a pillow worked in a needlepoint unicorn design. It was a coarse copy of a tapestry Elizabeth had seen hanging in the Queen's palace. She picked up the heavy blue book.

"Mom said that the quickest way to find information about the Umberlands is to check the index." Ann showed Elizabeth the finely printed lists in the back of the book that more than covered her lap. "Look up 'Umberland.'"

Elizabeth turned to a similar index in the blue book, but her gaze returned again and again to the silent box. Perhaps she could surprise the boy when he came back to life.

"Here's Michael, Duke of Umberland." Ann turned quickly to a page inside and read for a moment as Elizabeth anxiously looked over her shoulder. "It only mentions him," she said with disappointment, turning the page. "But here's a picture. Look at the fancy clothes." She showed Elizabeth the portrait of a man in doublet and long hose, leaning against a tree, reading a book.

"'Tis Essex!" Elizabeth felt stunned. Here was her friend in a history of England. She struggled to comprehend the proof that she had somehow come to a time when her friend's life, and her own, was past.

"Do you really know that guy?" Ann asked.

"I do." As in a dream, Elizabeth searched the index of her own blue book. "Here is Father again!"

She quickly located the page and began to read. "How Father would laugh to hear about the so-called 'quarrel' between him and Essex! Father has tried to distance himself in public, but really they are the best of friends." Father always said that he valued his head, so he did his best to stay out of political schemes, but he loved his friends almost as much as his head. Elizabeth knew more than the author of the book she was reading.

She raced through the story of her friend and Father's, the charming, energetic Essex, and the crystal ball of Kathy's history book revealed his future to her. She gasped at what she saw, read on again, then clapped the book shut and threw it across the cold hearth.

"What's the matter?"

Elizabeth stared at the book and the ashes that had risen in a cloud around it and now sifted down to bury its blue cover.

"What is it?"

Elizabeth counted months on her fingers. "Four."

She dropped her hand into her lap, too shocked to cry. "In four months' time, Rob Devereux, my dear Essex, will be dead. In February, the Queen will execute him for rebellion and treason." Elizabeth shut her eyes. "And in three more years, my sweet old Queen will join him in the grave."

But of course this was foolishness. The Queen might be angry at her old friend, but the Queen had been angry at others and forgiven them. Surely she would command Essex to speak to her on his knees. She would banish him from court. But surely she would never behead him. Surely. She would never.

CHAPTER TWELVE

Charington in Flames

"HERE'S THE BOX of tissues." Ann pushed something into Elizabeth's lap. "You know. Like handkerchiefs. To blow your nose."

Elizabeth wiped her eyes and stared at the cold ashes on the hearth.

"Is it really true that they cut off people's heads?"

Elizabeth nodded. "Too true." She went to the hearth, weighed down by her new knowledge. Silently she fished out the book with one finger and her thumb, blew away ashes that clung to the blue cover, and brushed it with tissues.

She sat down again with Ann's garish pink robe pulled snug around her and her hands clasped on the book in her lap. "Essex. He would call me Poppet." She remembered Essex tousling her hair, bringing her sweetmeats, lifting her up in his arms, as affectionate as he had always been since she was a baby. "I feel I have, of a sudden, grown old."

Ann patted Elizabeth's knee.

"I do not think I like knowing the future." Elizabeth brushed at the ashes left on the book. "Can it be that I really have come through time so far from home? How can I look at Rob Devereux again, knowing what will befall him? Go back I must, of course. I must take the blessed medicine to my mother."

Suddenly frantic, she turned again to the index in the blue book. "U." Her finger moved down the page, and she muttered at what she saw there. "Umberland, Andrew. John, Duke of. Michael." She clapped the book shut again. "No Margaret! No Catherine! No Elizabeth! This foolish scribe hardly mentions Father, and he thinks Margaret too inconsequential for his book! Perhaps he is wrong about Rob Devereux as well." She heard her shrill voice echo in the fireplace and trail off up the chimney.

The girls sat quietly, stunned into silence by Elizabeth's passion. Then Ann asked, "Did you hear what you said a minute ago? That you would take the medicine back to your mother?"

"Yes," said Elizabeth firmly. "That is what I intend to do."

"But how will you go back?"

Elizabeth shut her eyes. "I do not know, but I must find a way. My mother needs my help."

Very gently, no longer blustering and chattering, Ann took the blue book away and put another larger volume in Elizabeth's lap. "Try this one. Maybe a different historian is wiser. Besides, this book has colored pictures."

Ann and Elizabeth read first in one book and then in another. Once Ann held up a picture of the majestic Queen for Elizabeth to see. "Nothing! Nothing here about Charington House or you. Nothing but portraits of this stern Queen of yours. And boring paintings of the English ships that fought against the Spanish Armada." She flipped the book shut. "I never even heard of the Armada before. Now I don't ever want to hear about it again."

Elizabeth nodded. "Your historians seem to think that the Armada and the Queen and Shakespeare's plays are the only things that matter in my time." Elizabeth stroked Prissy from head to tail, enjoying the purr that vibrated under her hand.

"Same thing in books about America," said Ann. "Who ever heard whether Columbus or George Washington had kids?" She took the next book from the stack and read the title aloud. "'*Daily Life in Queen Elizabeth's Court.*'"

Ann paused and turned to her friend. "Tell the truth, Elizabeth. Do you really know the Queen? Do you really go to fancy balls and wear velvet dresses all the time?"

"I do speak the truth, with all my heart. I know the Queen very well, indeed. But not even she wears velvet all the time."

Ann stared at the fireplace.

"What is it?" asked Elizabeth.

"I can see myself dancing with a prince," said Ann dreamily. Then she suddenly laughed. "Me, dancing with a prince!" She turned a page in the book on her lap. "I hope we find something soon. Mom'll be coming home, and we'll have to help with dinner."

The girls read quietly again until Ann broke the silence. "Elizabeth!" She pointed at the page. "Here it is!" She slammed the book shut on her fingers to save her place.

Holding the book in her arms, Ann hurried to her mother's desk and rummaged with one hand through a drawer until she found a pad of paper and a pencil.

Back on the sofa, Ann picked up Raggedy Ann and opened the book, keeping the open page secret. "Describe your coat of arms," she commanded.

"'Tis a rampant stag and a panther, with a cluster of acorns and oak leaves. You saw it on the back of my music box." Elizabeth found the music box in the pocket of the robe and held up the carved walnut case for Ann to see. "I keep it with me, and Mariah, in case I should find my way suddenly back to Charington." She patted her other pocket. "And the medicine is here."

"Shut your eyes and tell me what the stag looks like."

"One branch of his antlers is broken."

"And the colors?"

"A banner of blue and gold, with oak leaves traced in red."

Ann looked at Elizabeth with wonder. "I know it's farfetched, just as Mom and Dad said, but sometimes I almost believe you. Here." She handed the paper and pen across Prissy. "Here's another test. We'll prove once and for all whether or not you're a princess."

"I am no princess." Elizabeth spoke with a newly felt calm. At that moment, it didn't matter what anyone else believed; Elizabeth herself knew the truth. "Only the daughter of a duke."

"Well, whatever you are. Can you draw a picture of your house? Charington House." Ann paged through the book and found her place again.

With the skill of a trained artist, Elizabeth began to draw the long front of Charington. "There are thirty windows on the second story," she said, "and four fewer on the bottom, because of the entryway. I counted them last summer." With a hand guided surely by memory, she penciled in the windows and then began work on the roof. "Although the house has sixty chimneys, one may see only twelve of those from the front. They are located . . . about here . . . and here."

She drew rapidly, a small smile on her face, with the pleasure anyone might feel who had come upon a photograph of a beloved place.

"Your house is huge," said Ann, as she watched the drawing come to life. "Where did you learn to draw like that?"

"My tutor gives me drawing lessons. Here is the gravel drive," Elizabeth went on. "And here the staircase down to the lagoon, which Father built last year." She looked at Ann for a moment. "The workmen diverted a sluice of water from the Thames," she explained. "Everybody told him that it couldn't be done, but that only made Father more determined to design a way."

"Why in the world do you need so many chimneys?" Ann opened the book to the place she had marked with her finger, and looked at something inside. "I can see how big your house is, but a few furnaces should be enough to heat it."

"Furnaces?" said Elizabeth. "Charington is very modern. Each room is heated by its own fireplace."

Ann nodded, and looked at the book again. She began to count something under her breath. "Right again. Twelve." She stared at Elizabeth in silence. Then she held the book up dramatically for Elizabeth to see. "Look!" she said, as if Elizabeth were not already wide-eyed.

For there on the page was a painting in black and

white of her own dear Charington. And there beneath the picture of her house was a colored portrait of Michael and Margaret and their daughter. Margaret held a little baby in her arms, a baby dressed in a christening gown that hung almost to the floor.

Elizabeth gasped, and she thought her heart had stopped as she struggled for composure. "Those are certainly my parents, looking a little older than they really are. And this girl resembles me. But who is the baby?"

"Look on the chair beside the girl."

Elizabeth looked closely at the picture. "The music box," she said, but she was looking at something else in the shadow of the chair. It seemed to be a doll, one with a blue dress and striped stockings and a shock of red hair.

Elizabeth looked again at the girl in the portrait. "See how tall she stands. 'Tis as if she had put aside childish things and become a young woman."

"Yes," said Ann excitedly. "That's exactly what I thought. But look at the date painted at the bottom of the portrait."

"1605. Why, in 1605, I shall be fourteen years old. I shall be a young woman." Elizabeth read the caption under the portrait. "'Michael and Margaret, Duke and Duchess of Umberland, and their children, John and Elizabeth.'" Then the sheriff had been right. Her mother would indeed survive the illness Elizabeth had left her with. And if Margaret should bear a son, the family line would continue, just as the sheriff said it had until "it petered out in the eighteenth century."

"In your time, everything was so beautiful," Ann said. She smoothed her sweatshirt with the palms of her hands. "Are the gold and pearls on your dresses real?"

"Yes, all real." Elizabeth looked in wonderment at the portrait of her own future, remembering the day when she broke her mother's most precious vase. She had left a note of apology that said, "I am nothing like I will be when I grow up."

She had written those words with a confidence she had not felt; she had not been sure what she would be. She imagined herself beautiful and calm and responsible enough not to break her mother's treasures, but how could anyone know what she would be in the secret, dim future? Now she looked at a portrait that was like a strange mirror reflecting back the years ahead, and saw herself beautiful and self-possessed. Perhaps she would be responsible too.

"1605." Ann interrupted Elizabeth's thoughts and began quickly to search the page for something. "Listen! This is the part I read first. It's terrible, but it tells you for sure that you returned to your own time.

"'Charington,'" Ann read, "'was one of the finest houses owned by Elizabethan courtiers. It unfortunately burned to the ground in 1607 when a candle fell into a bundle of tinder, setting the wood paneling and the carpets and draperies alight.'"

"Burned to the ground?" Elizabeth exclaimed. "Everything? Everything gone in smoke?"

"Not everything. The portrait survived, and something better too."

"Oh, do go on!"

Ann pointed to the line she was reading, and Elizabeth's voice joined Ann's. "'The Duke's fabulous collection of classical literature was a total loss, except for two volumes which his daughter Elizabeth rescued, Plutarch's *Lives* and Homer's *Odyssey*, books now held by the British Museum.'"

Ann looked at Elizabeth with triumph in her eyes. "Now listen to the best part. 'Elizabeth saved more than books that day. It was she who spread the alarm and who led her injured parents and young brother through the smoke to safety.'"

Elizabeth was silent as she tried to take in this strange story about her future and the world's past. She knew these events had not happened to her yet, but if they hadn't happened, how could they be in a book?

"Oh, Elizabeth. You were telling the truth!" Ann embraced her. "After supper," she said, "we'll figure out a way for you to go back home again so you can be there when the fire starts."

At last, someone believed all that Elizabeth knew of

herself, and more. She took Ann's hand and clung to it, her relief at finding an ally mixed with disbelief of her own about Essex and the fire and the baby named John.

Elizabeth looked out the window, far across the Iowa cornfields. It was not corn she saw, but Charington in flames. She saw her mother, as she had been when Elizabeth last kissed her, lying ill in the great canopied bed.

"Medicine," she said. "I must take the tonic back with me."

CHAPTER THIRTEEN

Outsmarting Dr. Davis

WHEN KATHY RETURNED HOME from work, Joe was already in the kitchen, washing his face and hands at the sink. Elizabeth and Ann nearly knocked them over with the energy of their excitement.

"Whoa!" Kathy put her briefcase on the kitchen table and brushed her hair back with her hands. "Talk one at a time so I can understand you."

"We found pictures – ," said Elizabeth.

"In the books you gave me – ," said Ann, leafing through the book for the proof.

"My parents and I and a baby brother who isn't even born yet – " Elizabeth pointed at the picture Ann was holding up.

"Her house and the Umberland coat of arms." Ann held the drawing of Charington in front of Joe, who, blinded by soapy water, was standing in the bathroom door drying his eyes on a towel.

"Hold on." Squinting, Joe examined the drawing closely, pointing at identical details in the book. "It's remarkable, all right, how well you know the house, Elizabeth. I guess you must have come across this book somewhere before."

"No," said Elizabeth with certainty. "'Tis my memory of the house itself, and not the picture of the house. I can draw the rooms, as well, and show you where the chairs and chests do stand, and tell you what is in the chests." She leaned over Joe's arm and pointed. "My room is here, on the southwest corner of the house, where the windows catch whatever sun may shine."

Elizabeth had a fleeting memory of the splinter of sunlight that had fallen on her bed, the instant before she found herself standing in the McCormicks' pig-pen, blinded by the glare from the open door. She took Kathy's hand in her own. "I must go back to my home."

"You're desperately homesick." Kathy put her arm around Elizabeth's shoulders. "But 1600 is nearly four hundred years ago. Despite all these coincidences, you *couldn't* have come here from another time. There must be a simpler explanation."

"Now, Kathy," said Joe in his easygoing way. "Let's hear these girls out."

Elizabeth felt tears close to the surface. Kathy disbelieved her openly, while Joe, humoring her, doubted just as much. But perhaps one ally was enough, and Ann was talking now.

"Elizabeth's going to go back home."

"You have treated me most kindly, but my mother needs me," Elizabeth said.

"Well, you came here through the pigpen," said Joe. "Maybe you can go back by the same route."

"Wait a minute!" said Kathy. "You're feeling better, but you're not ready for a trip to England."

"My mother needs my penicillin," Elizabeth cried. "I cannot wait!"

"*You* need your penicillin," said Joe. "Never give your medicine to somebody else. Might not be the same sickness. Might not be the right medicine."

"She can ask Dr. Davis for more," said Ann with her hand on Elizabeth's arm. "You said she's coming for supper tomorrow."

"She'll never give you medicine for a patient she hasn't seen," said Kathy. "Playing 'Time Machine' is one thing, but playing doctor with real medicine is another. You mustn't try to leave here. Let us find your family for you."

Suddenly Kathy looked up at Joe. "Why are we talking in this ridiculous way? Why encourage her hope?" Then she turned back to Elizabeth. "You must know, dear, that we only want what's best for you."

Joe went on drying his face. "Well, there's no harm

in her trying to go back, is there, Elizabeth? As long as you don't wander off the farm again." He smiled. "It'll give you girls something to do."

"You're right, Joe," Kathy said, turning again to Elizabeth. "There's no harm in trying. And no need for us to settle the question of whether you might succeed."

Kathy tried to give her a hug, but Elizabeth eluded it. She would not be taken in by the gesture of a woman who had no faith in her.

After Kathy had tucked the girls into bed, kissed them, and turned out the light, they lay in silence, watching the blue shadows of tree branches cast by the sailing moon. This day's events would take some sorting out.

"My mother," said Elizabeth at last. "How can I get medicine for my mother?"

Ann reached across the space between the beds, and Elizabeth touched her hand.

As the shadows moved on the wall, the girls thought and talked. "We could tell Dr. Davis the whole story," said Elizabeth.

"We could, but I think Mom's right. Shanasha will never give your mother medicine unless she sees her blood count." Ann propped herself up in bed on one elbow. "Mom and Dad think you're imagining everything, even though they found you. Even though they've seen your portrait in the book."

Ann and Elizabeth talked and thought and planned a strategy until drowsiness overtook them. They awoke early in the morning to talk and plot some more. All that day, while Ann was at school, Elizabeth rested. She read magazines about Ann's brave new world. She watched a puzzling game on TV, something called baseball and the World Series. Gradually, the things she had learned about the baby in her mother's arms, the death of Essex and the Queen, settled in her mind.

After school, Ann gave Elizabeth clean clothes; the jeans and the pink sweatshirt that matched Ann's were loose and warm. The girls sat on the bed with their legs tucked up like ruffians and considered the best way to trick Shanasha Davis. And when the doctor came to supper that evening, they knew what they must do.

The meal took forever as the adults savored the chicken and biscuits and talked about the corn. "I hear there's a bumper crop," said Dr. Davis.

"Yes," Joe replied with a satisfied nod, "I made a hundred and eighty bushels an acre off the back of the farm, where the soil's black as night down as far as you can dig."

The girls glanced sidelong at each other. "Here." Ann handed a full plate to Dr. Davis. "Have another biscuit."

"No thanks," said the doctor, gesturing with the

buttered and honeyed biscuit she was eating. "I notice all the farmers who come to town are wearing smiles on their faces."

"There's only one thing wrong with a bumper crop, Sharon," said Kathy. "When we've got one, everybody else does too. So many farmers have overflowing bins this year that the price is no good."

The girls toyed with their food, unable to eat, waiting for an opportunity to take Dr. Davis off alone to work their plan on her.

The doctor turned to Elizabeth. "You're looking more zippy than you were the other day, but most of your dinner is still on your plate. You need to drink lots of juice and milk. You need the protein in the chicken, too."

"She's homesick. And she's too excited to eat," said Ann. "We found the proof that she really did come from Queen Elizabeth's time."

"Did you now?" Sharon Davis smiled and glanced at Joe and Kathy.

"They turned up some remarkable coincidences in a book about the Elizabethan court," said Kathy. "There's a portrait hanging in the British Museum of the Duke of Umberland and his family. His daughter actually did bear a striking resemblance to our twentieth-century Elizabeth here."

"For goodness' sake," said Dr. Davis, watching Elizabeth closely.

Kathy's tone of voice and the doctor's darting glance showed Elizabeth that they were trying hard not to hurt or embarrass her and Ann. They still did not believe them, though. Elizabeth looked at Ann uneasily; surely the adults' doubts would not sway her faith in their plan. Ann idly stirred her potatoes and gravy with her fork without looking up.

"And that music box of yours really is an antique, isn't it, Elizabeth? The design on the back really is the Umberland coat of arms." Joe was interceding, filling the doctor in, but not believing any part of Elizabeth's story. Without help, she might never find medicine for her mother. She might never return home at all. She might be lost forever. Fear rose in Elizabeth's heart like a cold fog.

"What beats me," Joe went on, "is where she came by all this gear and how she learned so much historical lore. Why, she can even draw a true sketch of the Duke's house."

"All of a sudden you look so pale and tired, Elizabeth," said Kathy. "Do you want to lie down while we finish dinner?"

"Wait a minute," said Dr. Davis. "Where did your lovely music box come from, Elizabeth?"

"I had my music box as a gift from the Queen." How many times had she told people that? And still no one but Ann believed her.

"She makes perfect sense about the here and now,"

said Joe, "but her talk about the Queen and her home and family is as fantastic as ever."

Now they were talking about her as if she were absent or invisible. Elizabeth could bear their doubts no more. She stood without another word and left the kitchen on wobbly legs.

Ann followed Elizabeth silently up the stairs as Dr. Davis began to talk. "We don't have to solve the mystery right away," she said. "The child needs our comforting more than we need the facts. I may as well check her over now."

Dr. Davis brought her black medical bag with her. As she sat on the edge of Ann's bed, they held one another in a circle, their three heads touching.

"Believe me," Elizabeth whispered.

"I do," Ann replied.

"I'm listening," said Dr. Davis. She turned and opened the bag. Elizabeth shuddered when she saw the stethoscope and the microscope slides she had first encountered in the doctor's office. But standing in the bottom of the bag were bottles of medicine. She imagined her mother, up and walking and happy again, and she gathered her courage.

The doctor listened to Elizabeth's heart and shone the light into her ears and down her throat. She pierced her finger and spread a drop of Elizabeth's blood on one glass slide with the edge of the other, just as she had done in her office.

"Everything looks good," said Dr. Davis.

Elizabeth's mouth was cottony. Ann watched her intently, as if holding her breath, waiting for an opportunity.

"Are you taking your medicine?" the doctor asked. "Even though you feel well again, you need all of the penicillin tablets I gave you or the infection might come back."

Elizabeth hung her head and tried to look embarrassed.

"What's the matter?" said Dr. Davis.

"You might as well tell her the truth, Elizabeth," said Ann, just as the girls had planned. "She'll probably find out anyway. Besides, Shanasha is a very understanding doctor."

The girls looked at one another in silent, masked delight. They felt as if they could read one another's minds.

"Why are you buttering me up, Ann McCormick?" asked Dr. Davis.

"I lost my medicine," said Elizabeth hastily.

"How could you lose your medicine?"

"I dropped it in the toilet, so I threw it away."

"Oh, dear," said Dr. Davis. "That's gone forever, then. But I carry another bottle of penicillin in my bag." She looked at the labels on the plastic containers until she found the right one. "Let's see how many more you'll need." She counted days on her fingers.

Then she poured a handful of tablets and put them in an empty bottle, which she set on the table beside the bed. "I'll write out a label in a minute."

As she went into the bathroom to wash her hands, Elizabeth and Ann shot each other triumphant glances.

But a moment later, Dr. Davis came out of the bathroom with a stormy look on her face and Elizabeth's own bottle of penicillin tablets in her hand. "All right, girls. What's going on here?"

Elizabeth and Ann sighed. How could they have been so stupid? They had forgotten that the medicine bottle stood on the sink for anyone to see.

"Now we *have* to tell her the truth," said Ann.

"I must take the tonic home with me for my mother," Elizabeth said in a rush. "Her sore throat began a week before mine did. Now I fear she is dying."

"She'll have to see her own doctor, Elizabeth. I can't prescribe drugs for somebody I've never met."

"The alchemist came and gave her purgatives that made her so ill she nearly died," said Elizabeth with tears in her eyes. "The physician came with a basket of leeches. They bled her into a basin as well, and left her so weak she could not stand. We have no penicillin in London."

"But of course you do," said Dr. Davis. "Penicillin is available everywhere. And nobody is ignorant enough to use purgatives and leeches and bleeding to treat infections since Louis Pasteur discovered microbes and Alexander Fleming found that a penicillin spore had killed a dish of bacteria in his laboratory."

"You don't understand, Shanasha!" Ann said. "It isn't scientific! Elizabeth somehow came here from another time. We don't know how it happened, but here she is, and there her mother is, back where Elizabeth came from."

Dr. Davis shook her head. "What stories you girls tell." She absently picked up the music box that was lying on Elizabeth's bed and traced the inlaid-gold date with her fingertip. "1600," she said as she slowly turned the crank and the music began to flow. "You're right about the medicine they practiced back then, Elizabeth. Purgatives and leeches were all the medicine the physicians had."

She shook her head again. "I can't treat a patient I haven't examined."

"If Elizabeth's mother were dying in Alaska, far away from doctors, you could listen on the short-wave radio and tell the people what to do!" said Ann. "I read about that in a book."

Dr. Davis rubbed the carved walnut against her cheek and stared at Elizabeth. "Tell me about your mother's illness. The truth, girl."

"One day, her throat hurt so much she could hardly swallow, and she felt so ill she went to bed."

"Was her skin hot?" the doctor asked. "Did she complain of being chilled and ask for blankets? Did you see anything unusual on her skin?"

"How did you know?" Elizabeth stared at Dr. Davis. "She asked for fur coverlets and featherbeds even when her skin felt hot on my hand. And for a short time, I saw a red pattern on her skin."

"What happened then?"

"The ague. Her elbows ached, and she wept with the pain in her knees and ankles when she tried to stand."

"What else?"

"She gasped for breath, and her skin was gray, and she held her chest with her hand, for the pain."

"My dear," said Dr. Davis. "If your mother were in Alaska, I'd say on the radio that she probably had rheumatic fever, an illness related to the scarlet fever you've had. And I'd say that she needed penicillin."

She put her arm around Elizabeth and pulled Ann close. "But you tell me this farfetched, cock-and-bull story about a noble family in Elizabethan England. How can I treat a ghost who's been dead close to four hundred years? How can I give medicine to a child to carry through a fictitious time machine?"

"Wait." Ann ran down the stairs and came back carrying the book, with Prissy the cat on her heels. She quickly found the pages she had marked with scraps of paper. "Proof," she said, turning to the picture of

Charington. "Look at this drawing Elizabeth made for me before I showed her the one in the book."

Dr. Davis compared the drawing with the illustration. Then she looked at the portrait, turned to Elizabeth, and studied the painting once again. "The girl is older, but she more than resembles you, my dear. You're going to be a beauty." She pointed to the toys in the portrait. "And who might this be? She looks familiar."

Dr. Davis glanced around and found Raggedy Ann. "Yes. Proof," said Dr. Davis. "Raggedy Ann hadn't been thought of in 1605."

She stroked her chin and thought for a moment. "We'll have to tell Joe and Kathy that you have the medicine, of course. And they'll need to know that you're going to try to return where you came from."

Dr. Davis waited for the girls to nod agreement. "You must not take this medicine yourself, or give it to anybody but your mother," she went on decisively. "Give her four tablets each day – one at midnight, another at six in the morning, another at noon, and the last one at six in the evening. Make certain sure she takes every tablet, even after she feels better. Otherwise, the sickness might come back."

Dr. Davis wrote out her instructions and put them inside the container. "Tell your father her recovery will be slow. She'll need rest for a long time, and good food. She might be weak from a damaged heart." She embraced Elizabeth. "And tell him to barricade the doors against the alchemist and the leech."

She held Elizabeth out at arms' length and looked at her. "Who knows anything much about time? St. Augustine himself said that he could understand time only until he tried to explain it."

The doctor kissed Elizabeth on each cheek. "Blessings on your journey. If you can't figure out how to go back home, you must return the medicine to me." She put her fingertips on her temples and looked at the girls with a smile on her face. "And if you can, what in the world are we going to tell the sheriff?"

CHAPTER FOURTEEN

Playmates and Friends

*E*LIZABETH WAS WAITING on the lawn the next afternoon when Ann got off the school bus. She raced across the sunlit farmyard, calling "Come on! Come on!" as she dropped her backpack on the porch steps.

Ann ran toward the barn, yelling "Fly, pigeons!" so loud her voice echoed off the barn walls, and the pigeons did as they were bidden, rising in a flock from the ridge of the roof. Elizabeth chased after her, trying to imitate Ann's exuberance.

Suddenly Ann did a forward flip, then a cartwheel. She fluently moved into a handstand and walked several paces on her hands, pursuing Elizabeth, who retreated backward, laughing.

"Can you do gymnastics?" Ann said, panting and right-side-up again.

Elizabeth glanced sidelong at the house, half expecting Sukie to open the door and reprimand her for un-ladylike behavior. "Sukie would keep me in my room for a week if she caught me doing anything of the sort."

"Well, Sukie isn't here," said Ann.

Elizabeth plunged her hands into the front pouch pocket of her sweatshirt and toyed with Mariah and the bottle of penicillin she always carried now for her mother, in case lightning should strike again and carry her back home.

"What do you do for fun?" asked Ann.

"I have seen the jugglers turn themselves topsy-turvy at the Globe Theatre as the crowd comes in for one of Master Shakespeare's plays. And the street ur-chins teach one another such tricks."

She had never admitted to anyone that sometimes she envied the ragamuffins who ran in wild gangs through the streets of London, with no adults to scold them. But now Elizabeth felt a duty to defend her people's customs.

"Gentlewomen learn more delicate skills." She felt the little toss of her head. Ann might think her haughty, but Ann would never know the pleasure of sitting among women, talking about their lives and making beautiful things. "We learn to sew fancy stitches and to play music on the lute."

"Ooooooo, ex-citing," said Ann in the mocking tone that always made Elizabeth cringe. "Are you going to be a seamstress when you grow up?"

"The Queen herself is very clever at needlework," said Elizabeth. "I shall marry a nobleman and manage his house, like every other noblewoman." Elizabeth had never thought of doing anything else. Now she knew that there was nothing else for her to do. "And you, I suppose, will be a farmer's wife."

"Hah! Maybe I'll be a farmer, all by myself. Unless I'm a doctor, like Shanasha Davis. Maybe I'll be President."

"What's a president?"

"The President runs America, something like a king or queen, except the ordinary people choose the President," said Ann. "Do you want me to teach you how to turn a cartwheel like a born urchin?"

"Oh, yes!" said Elizabeth. "There's no Sukie to scold me now." She carefully set Mariah with the music box and the medicine in a clump of clean grass.

Ann showed her how to set her hands and how to kick off and let her body follow naturally. Elizabeth tried, and tried again, but every time she fell in a painful heap. "The harder I try," she wailed, "the more awkward I grow. You make it look so easy."

"It is easy, if you relax. You're too stiff. Think about something else, like falling off a log or playing scales on the lute." Ann turned another cartwheel to demonstrate. "Try singing a song this time."

So Elizabeth sang a song about the English navy defeating the Spanish Armada while she set her hands, kicked off, and felt her body following as naturally as if she had turned cartwheels before she learned to walk.

"I can do it!" she squealed, in an unladylike voice. "I can turn a cartwheel!" And she turned seven of them, one after another, to make sure she wouldn't forget.

"Imagine doing that in a velvet dress," said Ann.

"Yes, and farthingales and corsets. A corset would cut me in half at the waist if I bent more than this." Elizabeth did a dainty dance step, fluttering her eyelashes behind an imaginary fan.

She tucked her toys and her medicine into the pouch of her sweatshirt. Then she ran behind Ann into the barn and up the ladder to the haymow and scrambled up to the top of the stacked hay. Suddenly, with a wild whoop, Ann rushed past, slipping and sliding down the mound of hay. Elizabeth lunged for her, trying to prevent the nasty fall, but missed, and Ann plummeted into another pile of hay on the barn floor.

Elizabeth held her breath, thinking that Ann could never have survived such a fall.

But Ann picked herself up, laughing, with hay caught in her yellow hair, and called up to Elizabeth. "Come on. It's your turn."

"Oh, no, I couldn't."

"Of course you could. Just let go and slide. I'll catch you."

"I don't like sliding in hay."

"I'll bet you never tried it before. Just let yourself go."

Let herself go. How did one let oneself go? As easily as falling off a log or playing scales on the lute.

She laid Mariah gently in the hay and began to sing the song about the Spanish Armada. Her body started to slide on the slippery hay, gathering speed as she clamped her mouth shut and felt herself fall in silence out of the haymow, down, down through the air and into the springy haystack below. But the next time and the next and the next, she sang in a booming voice that echoed around the barn, until both girls fell exhausted into the piled hay in the mow.

They lay still and listened to the pigeons chortling in the rafters overhead. After a long time, Ann said, "Why are you so still?"

"I never heard myself shout before," said Elizabeth. Then, in a small voice, she said, "I almost wish I could stay."

"I'd like to go back with you, if it weren't for the plague and the beheading of Essex." Ann held her hand above her face and looked at her fingers in a beam of sunlight. "I'd like to have your velvet dresses and fancy balls and dinner with the Queen." She threw a handful of hay up into the air and watched it float back down. "Elegance."

"Life for peasants – "

"We're not peasants," Ann said. "We're farmers. We own this land. We worked to buy it."

"Farmers then. Life for farmers is not elegant. You would live in a hut on a nobleman's land. No electricity. No toilet. No penicillin."

"Okay. No elegance, none. But I get so bored alone here on the farm."

"If you're bored in London," said Elizabeth, "you can always go to a public execution. But Father won't let me go. He says executions are no place for ladies."

Elizabeth and Ann looked at each other and laughed. But, as Essex came to mind, sorrow rose in Elizabeth's chest. She thought of her mother, as she did a thousand times a day. How could she laugh and play when her mother lay so ill?

Dr. Davis had spoken to Kathy and Joe last night about the medicine, and the girls had listened on the stairs.

"I agree that it's a farfetched story," said Dr. Davis after listening to the McCormicks' doubts. "But it won't hurt to let her carry an extra bottle of penicillin around with her."

"Yes," said Kathy. "We don't have to believe her wild story to let her do that."

"And, as you say, Sharon," said Joe, "we can comfort her, whether we solve the mystery or not."

"Carrying the medicine will relieve her anxiety," said Dr. Davis. "If she could travel through time, she could help a mother ill with rheumatic fever. Of course, reason tells us that she can't, but I want to believe like a child that she can. If she tries and fails — well, we'll take care of her."

Now the girls lay in Ann's Iowa haymow, and Elizabeth was no nearer London than she had been last night, when Kathy and Joe had talked with Dr. Davis.

"How shall I ever go home?" Elizabeth cried. "I wished upon a star last night. I tried with might and main all day, while you were at school. I shut my eyes and imagined my bed. I prayed to Providence."

"Did you say any spells?" Ann touched Elizabeth's forehead with a stem of hay, as if it were a magic wand. "Come to think of it, I don't believe I know any spells. Do you?"

"People who say spells have been burned at the stake as witches all over Europe." Elizabeth shuddered at the terrible stories she had heard about the Inquisition. Thousands of people, many of them poor, old women, had died, accused of evil and unable to prove themselves pure.

"We don't believe in witches in Iowa, except on Halloween. We'll have to make up our own original spell."

"I have seen the herb woman call upon the four winds for grace," Elizabeth said. "But I could not hear her words."

"Show me."

Elizabeth turned toward the barn's north wall.

Elizabeth turned toward the barn's north wall.

"North Wind,
North Sea . . ."

She struggled to think of powerful things to say.

"Northern Lights,
Thy majesty,
Carry me home!"

Gooseflesh shivered up her arms as she spoke. Then she turned to the south.

"Don't forget Mariah." Ann handed Elizabeth the doll.

"South Wind,
South Sea . . ."

Elizabeth tried to think of holy powers that rhymed.

"And all the angels and
archangels in the firmament,
Deliver me!"

The words tumbled out. Maybe mistakes in rhyme and rhythm wouldn't matter.

"I thought of a spell," Ann whispered. "Try hocus, pocus, dominocus."

Elizabeth turned again.

"West Wind,
West Sea,
Hocus, Pocus, Dominocus,
Return me to my people."

She shut her eyes as she turned to the east, willing herself at home.

"East Wind,
East Sea . . . "

Elizabeth cast her mind back to the words with which the Archbishop bespoke his reverence for the sacred things in heaven and earth.

"Alpha and Omega . . . "

She faltered, trying to remember what the cook would say to keep the sauce from separating.

"By the Great Horn Spoon," whispered Ann, as if once again she were reading Elizabeth's thoughts.

"By the Great Horn Spoon," said Elizabeth solemnly. She shut her eyes and wished and willed and prayed and hoped all at once.

When she looked up, she still was standing in the haymow with Ann beside her, just as before. She lay down in the hay and stared bleakly at the dark rafters, while the pigeons cooed high above and the pigs squealed down below. "I shall never find my way."

"You give up too soon." Ann picked the hay out of her blond hair. "That's what happens when you let other people wait on you hand and foot."

"But I have tried all day. For naught."

The girls lay quiet until they grew sleepy. Elizabeth thought about all the strange things she had seen. The magical box with the boy inside. The silver bird streaking across the blue sky. She thought about electric lights and the amazing pictures in *Time* magazine.

"Tell me, Ann, what sort of jest or insult the *Time* pamphleteers mean when they say of the plain woman in blue, 'Queen Elizabeth will fly to Canada.'"

"Canada's a country in North America. Queen Elizabeth is the Queen of England now. I guess they named her after your Queen.

"But – *fly?*"

Ann laughed. "Can't you just see her, with wings in her back, swooping in and out of the clouds?" Glancing at Elizabeth, Ann shut down the laughter that bubbled as she talked. "Oh. I forgot. You don't know about airplanes. They're machines. Like cars. They fly through the air, and sometimes they leave a long white vapor trail behind them. The Queen will ride in an airplane."

Elizabeth remembered the silver bird with the long white tail. The silver bird was an airplane, then.

The pigs stirred and oinked below while the girls stared into the dark recesses at the top of the barn.

"Don't forget the portrait in the book," Ann said at last. "You were there for the portrait painter."

Hope rose up like a bird in Elizabeth's breast. "I'll try again tomorrow," she said, touching her forehead and her chest and each of her shoulders with the tips of her fingers. "Tomorrow."

Ann began to sing the song about the Spanish Armada, and Elizabeth joined in. Their hands clasped, playmates and friends, they slid down out of the mow and fell into the soft hay stacked on the floor of the barn below. Until tomorrow.

CHAPTER FIFTEEN

A Splinter of Sunlight

WHEN SATURDAY DAWNED in brilliant golden sunlight, the girls were ready to try again.

Elizabeth dressed in all her finery. As the velvet gown, clean and bright again, went over her head, the playfulness of the past few days fell away.

"I shall remember the McCormicks always," she said. She tucked her mother's bottle of medicine into one pocket of her skirt, and her own bottle into the other.

"Now don't start that noble brat routine again, just because you're wearing velvet." Ann tied her sneaker as she talked. "If you feel yourself turning into Miss High-and-Mighty, just look at your feet."

Elizabeth looked in the mirror on the back of Ann's closet door. Instead of the gold-embroidered velvet slippers that the pigpen had spoiled forever, Ann's outgrown sneakers stuck out under her beautiful gown.

"What will Sukie say? 'Lady Elizabeth, wherever in the world did these urchin slippers come from?'" Elizabeth began to snicker, and then to laugh.

"'You must dress proper for your place in the world.'" Ann laughed too, continuing Sukie's imaginary scolding. "'None of these ragamuffin clodhoppers for milady.'"

"Looks like you're all ready to play the princess and the pauper," said Joe when the girls came into the kitchen for breakfast.

Ann went along with her father's joke. "Yes, Pop," she said. "That's right. We're going to play queens and kings in our pigsty after breakfast." Everybody laughed, but Elizabeth and Ann exchanged an uncertain glance that stopped the laughter in their throats.

In the barn that morning, Ann and Elizabeth looked over the fence at the sea of pigs. They jostled each other at the trough for food and wandered in waves in and out through the open door to the barnyard, grunting and snuffling, crowding and climbing over one another. Near the pen, the odor was so strong Elizabeth almost thought it might be visible in the air.

"I was standing precisely there, in the corner, when I found myself in your barn — there where the scrawny pig is huddled," said Elizabeth, as if remembering a dream. "Perhaps he is the one that greeted me like Puck."

"Maybe the runty pig was part of the magic. What else?"

"That lamp was burning above me later when I awoke from my swoon and found myself lying on those hay bales."

"But that was after, Elizabeth. What happened at the beginning?"

"My eyes were closed when first I smelled the pigs and heard the squeaking hinges as your father opened the door. I held Mariah in the crook of this arm and the music box in the other hand."

"You stand in the corner of the pigpen, and I'll open the door."

Each girl looked intently at the other's face, as if to memorize its features. "It just sank in," said Ann. "If we're able to send you back, we'll never see each other again."

"And if we're not," said Elizabeth so quietly she could barely hear herself over the pigs' noise, "I'll never see my parents again."

Their fierce embrace took away their breath.

"Farewell." Elizabeth dabbed her nose with the lace-edged handkerchief she had in her sleeve.

"Good-bye." Ann wiped her eyes with the back of her hand.

Elizabeth held out her doll to Ann. "Keep Mariah, and remember me."

"Take Raggedy Ann for the portrait painter," said Ann. She tucked her doll under Elizabeth's arm.

Elizabeth pulled Joe's barn boots over her sneakers and climbed the fence. She stood beside the runty pig, with the rag doll in the crook of one arm and the music box in the other hand. She checked the pockets of her skirt and felt the container of medicine Dr. Davis had given her. Then she shut her eyes.

"Ready," she said.

"Say hello to Queen Elizabeth for me," Ann called.

Elizabeth heard the hinges squeal, and she opened her eyes, expecting to see the blue velvet curtains around her bed at home. Disappointment weighed her down, for the pigs still swarmed around her. And Ann still stood at the barn door, waiting for something to happen.

"There was music playing. My own music." Elizabeth turned the crank on the beautiful carved music box. "Now try again." She shut her eyes as the Summermusic poured out its tinkling song above the rough voices of the pigs.

The music tinkled across the barn. The door screeched again. But when she looked about her, Elizabeth still stood in the midst of a herd of pigs, stuck in the McCormicks' Iowa barn.

"Perhaps it was the slippers." Elizabeth looked

down at Joe's rubber boots. "Perhaps the slippers were like seven-league boots that could carry me to this end of the earth. And the slippers are gone."

"Maybe you're not standing in exactly the right spot," said Ann.

"I felt so woozy, I'm not certain, after all." Elizabeth moved a step to her left. "Try again."

Time after time, all morning long, Elizabeth and Ann tried to make the magic work, adjusting little things in the hope of discovering the key. They tried and failed until lunchtime. After lunch, they tried again. The harder they tried, the more disappointed they felt. The more disappointed, the more they criticized one another.

"Maybe you're not holding the doll right," said Ann.

"Maybe you don't move the squeaky door quickly enough," said Elizabeth.

"Maybe you dreamed the whole thing."

"Maybe you should keep your mouth still."

They bickered until they both began to cry.

"I'm afraid we'll do everything wrong," said Elizabeth, "and I'll never see my mother and father again."

"I'm afraid we'll do everything right," said Ann, "and I'll never see you again. Let's stop thinking about it and play princess and pauper."

"You be the princess," said Elizabeth.

"You be the pauper," said Ann.

[124]

So Elizabeth took off the boots. The girls sat in the loose hay that was piled on the barn floor and played dolls, Ann speaking in an English accent for Lady Mariah, and Elizabeth adopting an Iowan's speech for Raggedy Ann.

They pretended that paupers and princesses might love one another. They played that ragamuffins and ladies might be best friends. They made up a story about a farmer's daughter dancing at a nobleman's ball and being accepted as a princess.

"We ought to have music at our ball," said Elizabeth, winding the crank on her music box.

As the music poured out, it seemed to rise above the snuffling grunts of the pigs and fill the barn. The door screeched open. Elizabeth looked up to see Joe Mc-Cormick silhouetted in the sun. He stepped inside, just as he had on that other day, and a blinding splinter of sunlight struck Elizabeth full in the face.

The next instant, she heard the brass rings on her velvet curtains squeak across the brass rails above her head.

She opened her eyes and saw Sukie's round face looking down at her, blocking the sunlight that was bright behind her. "Here, Lady Elizabeth, try another sip of broth."

"The sun," said Elizabeth. "Joe and the sunshine were the key."

CHAPTER SIXTEEN

Reunion

THE SUMMERMUSIC SPILLED out of the carved walnut box in Elizabeth's hand. At the foot of the bed, her dog Puck stood with his ears pricked, curious and alert.

Sukie pulled the wolfskin coverlet back. "Wherever did those ragamuffin slippers come from? They smell of the sty." She wiped the sneakers with a cloth. "Have you been playing with the servant girls again?"

"The girls have not come near since you sent me away from them, but I shall invite them to play tomorrow." Elizabeth climbed down from the high bed. Sukie had not changed a whit in her absence. "And I shall ask Father to give them warmer rooms and better food. I've been journeying, Sukie, to a land stranger than any country in books."

"The fever has addled your brains, my girl. You've been asleep no more than five minutes."

"The fever is gone. I am well, Sukie." Elizabeth left the music box playing on the bed and placed Sukie's hand on her brow.

As she remembered the smoking carriages that sped across the countryside faster than horses could ever run, however, she began to doubt her own wits. She thought of Kathy, a woman tutor at a university who dressed sometimes in trousers; surely no woman had ever behaved so boldly. She thought of the dark-skinned physician with the strange name she had chosen herself. Perhaps Elizabeth had dreamed the Mc-Cormicks and Dr. Davis.

Then she remembered how urgently she had needed the doctor's help. "My mother, Sukie. How does my mother fare?"

"Don't be silly," said Sukie, avoiding the question. "Your fever can't be gone so suddenly. You were burning hot a moment ago. Back to bed with you now!"

As Puck pranced behind her, grinning and panting his delight, Elizabeth hurried to the door, leaving the speechless Sukie behind her. She had disobeyed Sukie!

She hiked up her skirts and ran down the long, oak-paneled gallery, noticing the satisfying way her sneakers struck the carpet and the easy grace of her movement. Below the portrait of an ancestor who looked down his long nose at her, she turned an almost perfect cartwheel, and then ran on.

Near her mother's chamber stood the cabinets of her father's favorite books. Elizabeth imagined Charington in flames. She thought of Ann, who would be gone while almost four centuries passed, but who was alive in her heart today. She would greet the Queen for that peasant girl who could summon such power with the flick of a switch or the turn of a key as no queen had ever commanded.

Then Elizabeth pushed past the servants who clustered at her mother's door and hovered around the bed. Puck leaped up on the Duchess's pillow and licked her pale face before Dinah, the maid, could brush him away.

"Where have you been, my dear girl?" whispered Elizabeth's mother. Her eyes were half closed, as if it tired her to hold the lids open. "I heard the servants talking in the hallway. I feared you might be ill."

Elizabeth dropped Raggedy Ann on the bed, fell into her mother's arms, and laid her own cool cheek against the woman's hot one. The sun shone through the stained glass coat of arms that was mounted in the window. The light poured across the bed in pools of gold and scarlet, green and deep, deep blue.

"I *was* ill, Mother," said Elizabeth, taking the medicine from her pocket. "But I am better now. And so shall you be tomorrow." More confident than she had ever been, she shook one tablet out, closed her mother's fingers around it, and nestled the closed hand between her own two palms like a bird.

Dinah stepped forward with her arms outstretched, as if to protect her mistress, but the Duchess stopped her with a gesture.

The sunlight warmed their faces as Elizabeth's eyes held her mother's gaze. Time seemed to stop for a long moment. "I believe you," said the Duchess. "I will be better." She fixed her eyes on the maid. "A glass of wine, Dinah."

It was as simple as that. Without any questions, without even knowing all that had happened, her mother simply believed her.

Dinah propped the Duchess up among her pillows and helped her swallow the tablet with wine from a crystal goblet.

Elizabeth took a deep shuddering breath, sank onto her mother's soft shoulder, and wept. Her mother held her gently while the servants whispered at the edge of the room and Puck paced the floor, his claws tap-tapping on the burnished oak.

"This is not Mariah," said the Duchess when Elizabeth had cried out all the tears she had left to cry. "Who is this little poppet?" She tousled the doll's red hair.

"Meet Raggedy Ann, Mother."

Elizabeth made the doll stand and curtsy on the coverlet and watched a smile light her mother's eyes. She brushed a strand of damp hair back from the pale forehead.

And then Elizabeth put the calico doll of a farmer's daughter in the Duchess of Umberland's arm, where the baby named John would someday lie.